"Andrea's starting to heal. Thanks to you."

Brynn's anxiety was still strong. "Partially. Some of it's in her. But the most important step is still up to you."

Jake looked puzzled. "And you don't think I'll do my part?"

Wanting so much for Andrea, Brynn battled between diplomacy and truth. "I know you'll do everything in your power right now because you've nearly lost her. But what about later on? Will the next project in Kenya mean more than Andrea's sense of stability?"

"That was a low blow."

"I didn't mean it to be. I'm just trying to be realistic. Your job takes you far away. And I don't think Andrea can bear that anymore."

He blinked. "You're saying I have to choose between my career and my daughter?"

Dear Reader,

In the life of a writer, fact and fiction occasionally race along hand in hand. And when emotion begs to join them, a story grows. Such was the case in *For the Sake of His Child*.

Blessed with the world's most wonderful friends, I've shared some of their generosity and experiences. Perhaps you'll recognize yourself in the pages. Friends reaching out to friends. What could be better? Unless maybe it's the love such friends find with the men in their lives. Men we cherish as we shop, talk endlessly over lunch and, even better, when we go home at night.

Please join me as I celebrate the unmatched joys of romance, friendship, single parenting and the quest for that one special love.

And to my own Mr. Right, keep the lights on, sweetheart. I'll be home soon.

Sincerely,

Bonnie K. Winn

For the Sake of His Child

Bonnie K. Winn

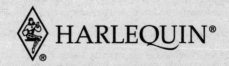

HARLEQUIN®

TORONTO • NEW YORK • LONDON
AMSTERDAM • PARIS • SYDNEY • HAMBURG
STOCKHOLM • ATHENS • TOKYO • MILAN • MADRID
PRAGUE • WARSAW • BUDAPEST • AUCKLAND

ISBN 0-373-71199-9

FOR THE SAKE OF HIS CHILD

www.eHarlequin.com

Printed in U.S.A.

To Jean Baker, for friendship, for giving, for sharing,
for always caring. I miss you, Texas girl.

And to Laura Shin, thank you.

Books by Bonnie K. Winn

HARLEQUIN SUPERROMANCE
 898—THE WRONG BROTHER
 964—FAMILY FOUND
1019—SUBSTITUTE FATHER
1139—VANISHED

Don't miss any of our special offers. Write to us at the
following address for information on our newest releases.

Harlequin Reader Service
U.S.: 3010 Walden Ave., P.O. Box 1325, Buffalo, NY 14269
Canadian: P.O. Box 609, Fort Erie, Ont. L2A 5X3

PROLOGUE

GLANCING IN THE REARVIEW mirror, Kirk Alder accelerated. The same dark green car remained close behind. The one that had tailed him from his studio.

Searching his memory, Kirk was almost positive the car hadn't been there before then. Not at the house, not at—

The deceptively fast Cadillac sped even closer.

Kirk reached for his cell phone. Cursing, he realized he'd left it behind at the studio, stashed in his camera bag. His mission had been so urgent he hadn't bothered with either.

Speeding up again, he wished he'd driven the Eclipse. The van's steering was clumsy and he didn't want to try any evasive maneuvers with the boxy vehicle. But it was Brynn's day out with Sarah. His wife and daughter loved the sleek lines of the Eclipse and they'd taken off for a day of shopping early that morning. And at the time he hadn't thought he'd have to evade a pursuer.

He glanced ahead on the freeway, spotting the exit he needed not too far away. Switching lanes at the last minute, he hoped to outwit the driver behind him. But the Cadillac stuck right behind him on the two-lane overpass.

It was time—past time—to talk with the police. He'd already waited too long. The police station was close.

A slow-moving eighteen-wheeler hogged the right lane, the one he had to be in to exit. Swearing, he looked to the left, hoping to pass the truck and speed ahead.

But the dark green Cadillac was still on his tail.

Before he could guess the driver's intention, the Cadillac slammed into the side of the van.

Kirk wrenched the steering wheel, trying to regain control. The van swayed on the high overpass.

Trapped behind the huge truck as he was, with the Cadillac boxing him in, there was no escape.

Desperately clenching the steering wheel with

all his strength, he tried to prepare for the next blow. This time the heavy car made a direct hit on the driver's-side door.

The sounds of tearing metal and shattering glass barely penetrated, blocked out by his last conscious thought: *It wasn't supposed to end this way! God, please let Brynn understand... please.*

CHAPTER ONE

Two years later, Walburg, Texas

THERE WAS A TIME when Brynn Alder had not been sad. A time before her life had been stolen. A time when she had reason to be happy.

Tall French doors stood ajar, opening onto the cobbled brick terrace. Black and white chickadees perched in the huge, aged oak tree, sharing morsels from the well-stocked feeder. As Brynn watched, a blue jay swooped toward them and they darted away. Sometimes, when all was still, the chickadees tentatively breached the boundary between their world and hers, hopping inside from the terrace, crossing the warm wood floor of her studio. They always made her smile.

Although Brynn had known the Texas Hill Country was beautiful before she'd moved here nine months earlier from San Antonio, her true appreciation hadn't developed until she'd settled in this house, drawn by the security it offered.

"Brynn, I'm going to get it this time," thirteen-year-old Emily insisted, panting as she tried to shape the slippery clay. It was time for the child to go home, to move past her troubles now that she had the coping skills she'd learned from Brynn. But not before she had one more try at the potter's wheel.

"Savor the feel of the clay in your hands," Brynn reminded her. It was the sensation, not the end result, that she wanted the girl to carry with her. Brynn closed her eyes, picturing not Emily, but her own daughter, Sarah, sitting at the wheel, a determined, expectant expression on her young face.

"Rats!" Emily interrupted the fantasy. "I blew another one." She held up a lumpy, shapeless object. "You're right. This isn't for everybody."

Brynn smiled gently, glad Emily would take away this important concept. Ignoring the emptiness in her heart, she reached for the piece of clay. "And learning that lesson makes this a wonderful memento of our time here together. May I keep it?"

A gigantic smile erupted on Emily's freckled face. "You really want to keep it?"

"Absolutely!" Brynn glanced at the clock on

the studio wall. "But now you have to pack." She had given in to Emily's request for one last walk, horse ride and session at the wheel. "Your parents should be here any minute."

"Okay."

Emily was a changed child. When she'd come to Brynn six weeks earlier, there had been no trace of a smile and no willingness to obey the simple rules Brynn insisted upon. It was ironic, her ability to read what other people's troubled children needed. If only she'd been so attuned to her own.

It was too difficult to go there, to relive the pain and loss. Instead, she followed Emily up the stairs, then detoured to her own room. Quickly Brynn exchanged her smock for a fresh T-shirt. She made few concessions to ceremony these days, since the remote location of the house seldom made them necessary. There were times it seemed she lived on the edge of the world. And despite the counsel of family and friends, she needed the solitude.

Loneliness wasn't a factor. Brynn knew she'd be equally alone in a crowded room. When she'd lost the ones she loved, a chasm had rent her soul. And no one could fill that void.

One of her beloved dogs, a Border collie

named Virgil, pushed his muzzle into her hand. She patted his silky head and his tail wagged in silent support as they walked down the stairs together.

Brynn had only enough time to fix some iced tea before the doorbell rang. The Hills, Emily's parents, could scarcely contain their anxiety.

But before Brynn could reassure them, Emily rushed down, her shoes making a noisy clatter on the wooden stairs. Running forward, she hugged her parents eagerly.

Surprise changed to gratitude as the Hills returned Emily's embrace, the room filling with enthusiastic voices.

A few minutes later, Emily's father still looked stunned as he glanced toward Brynn. "I don't know what to say."

"Enjoy your beautiful daughter," Brynn replied.

After accepting thanks, she watched the trio get into their car, then waved until they were out of sight. Once back inside, with the door closed, she found that the silence seemed louder than the noise the happy family had made. Only the clicking of Virgil's toenails broke the stillness.

Brynn strolled through the studio and onto the terrace. The house was too quiet, as it always was when a child left. And this one had stayed longer than most. As a result, Brynn was behind in her work. Contracts to three galleries had yet to be filled and she couldn't afford to lose the work. However, once the commissioned pieces were completed, she needed to rest. She couldn't mentor another child unless she had some down-time first.

Sitting in a comfortable, deep rocker, she surveyed the open green field before her. Her other three dogs were playing in the long grass, chasing rabbits or each other. Virgil was the one who glued himself to her side, keeping watch. Still, all the animals had adjusted well to the move. And to think less than a year earlier she'd had no pets. Now she couldn't imagine not having them around.

Virgil had been a gift from her best friend, Julia Ford. Worried about Brynn after Sarah's death, Julia had brought over the faithful dog. Unable to face the responsibility of having to care for another living creature and perhaps failing it, Brynn had determinedly headed for the shelter where Julia had purchased the dog, intending to return him. However, as she walked the aisles of caged animals, her tender heart had betrayed her.

Instead of returning Virgil, Brynn had brought home three additional dogs destined for destruction that day, along with two cats marked for a similar fate. And now they were her family.

A flash of sable surfaced in the field and she smiled. Shamus, her big, rambunctious setter mix, was galloping away from his smaller playmates. Brynn was indebted to her friend for far more than her pets. This was Julia's ranch—loaned to Brynn without hesitation or limitations.

Brynn's cell phone rang, interrupting her musing. She considered ignoring it, but knew she no longer had that luxury. The ranch phone rarely rang. Julia's visits were sporadic and most callers knew that the cell phone was the best way to reach Brynn.

The man's authoritative voice was one she didn't recognize, and his request one she was hoping to avoid.

She listened to him for a few moments. "I'm sorry, Mr....is it McKenzie? But I really can't take on another child at this time." Even now, exhaustion seeped through her bones. Helping a child took every bit of her limited emotional reserves.

"I was told you are the best," McKenzie responded.

Hearing determination in his tone, she winced, knowing how desperate some parents were for help. "I appreciate the compliment—"

"It's not a compliment. I wouldn't be bothering you if I had an alternative. I'm not crazy about sending my child away. But she needs you."

Brynn swallowed, hating to refuse, but knowing she had to. Battered by the events of the past year, her emotions were fragile. Although she volunteered willingly, she knew her limits. "Mr. McKenzie, the same people who recommended me can find you someone else."

"You have a unique approach, Mrs. Alder. No one else takes a child on a one-to-one basis. Group programs haven't helped my daughter. She's been in the highly recommended ones and the mildly recommended ones. They didn't make a dent."

"I'm sorry, Mr. McKenzie."

"This can't be discussed on the phone," he replied. "I can be at your place tomorrow—"

"No!" Fear made the word a screech. She calmed her voice. "As I said, I can't help her. Goodbye, Mr. McKenzie." She shut the phone, unwilling to hear more. Feeling the tightness in her throat, she made herself breathe more slowly.

Brynn had reluctantly given her phone number to Julia, family and a few doctors, but she'd never divulged her new home's location. Even her mail went to a post office box in San Antonio, which Julia checked. Her friend alerted her to anything that needed an immediate response, then brought the mail when she visited. And so far, it had worked. No one had bothered her here.

Breathing normally now, Brynn rubbed Virgil's ears. "I'm being ridiculous," she told the dog. "There's no way Mr. McKenzie or anyone else can find us here."

Still, she felt better once she'd rounded up all the pets and securely locked them inside for the evening.

THE FOLLOWING MORNING Jake McKenzie wasn't in any better humor, having driven through San Antonio's rush hour and then another three hours to the outlying edge of the Hill Country.

As chief engineer of worldwide Canyon Construction, he had grappled with seemingly impossible projects—bridges that spanned massive distances, skyscrapers that defied earthquakes and mammoth construction sites hundreds of miles from civilization. But his twelve-year-old daughter, Andrea, was beyond his scope.

He slowed the car as he studied the sprawling ranch-style house. It didn't look particularly re-markable. But the woman who lived there was reported to be more than remarkable. The parents of a child she'd helped had raved about Brynn's success with their troubled daughter, so Jake had convinced a friend to put him in touch with Mrs. Alder.

He parked beneath a tall oak tree, and as he left the car, it was so quiet Jake wondered if she was home. The garage was set to the side and behind the low house. Its doors were shut firmly, concealing whether a car was inside.

Climbing the steps to the wide front porch, he strode to the door and knocked firmly. The deep quiet was shattered. Dogs barked madly, and something smacked the other side of the door. One of the dogs, he guessed. But he didn't back away. He'd fight a pack of wolves if it meant helping Andrea.

As the yelping continued, he heard a woman's voice through the noise. "Who is it?"

"Jake McKenzie."

"McKenzie?"

"We spoke on the phone yesterday."

For a moment all he could hear was the barking. Then she commanded the dogs to be quiet. "I told you then I couldn't help you, Mr. McKenzie."

"Are we going to continue talking through the door?"

Several more seconds passed. Then the door opened a few inches, but the chain remained in place.

He peered inside, but couldn't see much. The woman's face was shadowed. "I've driven for hours to see you, Mrs. Alder."

"Not at my invitation." Suspicion still filled her voice. "How did you find out where I live?"

"From the parents of a child you helped, Susan Cranston."

Brynn sucked in her breath. "That information is strictly confidential."

"I'm not here to solicit state secrets. I want to discuss my daughter."

When she didn't speak, he wondered if she was going to shut the door. However, she unhooked the chain, then opened the door wider.

"Come in," she said, although her face and stance eloquently illustrated her reluctance.

He quickly noted the well-worn look of the house, but his examination was cut short as four dogs rushed forward to sniff at him. "You have quite a few dogs."

"Yes."

No explanations, excuses or boasting about her pets. He followed as she walked down a few steps into a rustic, oak-paneled den. The high ceiling was crisscrossed with thick, heavy beams, but light flooded in through tall, wide windows. One wall, a huge fireplace dominating its center, was nearly all stone—river rock that matched the exterior. It looked like a man's room—probably her husband's.

She gestured to a tall-backed leather club chair. As he sank into its comfortable depths, Brynn perched on the edge of the nearby sofa. Clearly she wasn't anticipating a lengthy visit.

"I want to tell you about Andrea," Jake began, sensing he had to cram as much information as possible into the time allotted to him. "Her mother, Val, abandoned us more than a year ago. It devastated Andrea. Even though Val was far from an ideal parent, she'd been physically there for our daughter until then."

"And you?"

"My job takes me all over the world. I employ a small household staff, including a nanny, but that can't take the place of a parent."

"Does Andrea see her mother?"

Jake met her eyes. "No. Val walked away and hasn't looked back. Not surprising, since she never wanted a child. I've tried to make it up to Andrea, but nothing's worked. She withdrew when Val left. She's no longer interested in friends, certainly not school. Her straight A's have dropped to failing grades. I thought time would heal the worst of her pain, but it hasn't."

"There are good doctors—"

"I've tried psychiatrists, psychologists, counselors."

"It takes time, Mr. McKenzie. A child isn't like a work project that can be completed by a certain date."

He set his mouth in a grim line. "We're running out of time, Mrs. Alder."

Brynn's eyes widened in alarm. "Has she attempted suicide?"

"No. But she's stopped eating and...I'm afraid she's going to slip away."

"You need to find a program that's suited—"

"You're not listening, *Mrs. Alder.* As I told

you on the phone yesterday, Andrea doesn't respond to programs.''

"And I'm afraid you're not listening, Mr. McKenzie. I'm not prepared to take on another child right now. Perhaps in a few months—''

"By then it could be too late. The doctors have her drugged with medications that are supposed to help. Instead the pills make her numb. The solution isn't more drugs or another group. She needs dedicated one-on-one care.''

"Then perhaps that's what *you* should try.''

Jake could feel the tic in his jaw as anger kicked in. "Unfortunately, my success rate can't compare with yours.''

"And unfortunately, I have work that must be completed. I simply can't accept another child right now.''

Jake narrowed his eyes. "I'm prepared to triple the amount you charge, with a hefty bonus as well.''

Brynn stood up, flanked by her dogs. "I don't charge for working with children. Money isn't going to change my mind.''

He stood in turn. "You can name your price,'' he insisted, unable to accept that she wouldn't help his daughter.

Brynn gestured to the door. "Mr. McKenzie,

I'd be happy to get in touch with a doctor who's been very successful with deeply troubled teenagers, but now, I must insist that this conversation end.''

"I'm not giving up."

"I'm not expecting you to," she replied quietly. "Just realize I'm not the last stop in your search."

Again he met her eyes. "That's where you're wrong, Mrs. Alder."

As the door closed behind him, he could hear the locks immediately tumble into place, followed by the latching of the chain. It was a good three-hour drive home, but that didn't dissuade him. He'd never taken no for an answer and he wasn't going to start now.

INSIDE, BRYNN SLUMPED against the door, her breathing shallow, her pulse fluttering. Shock from the man's unexpected presence wasn't receding. Instead it worsened. If he could find her, how safe was this house? And why had the Cranstons disregarded their promise to keep her personal information private?

Virgil nudged her gently and she gave him a reassuring pat. When the dog's ears pricked up, she walked quickly to the window to see Jake

McKenzie's car driving away. Replaying his words in her mind, she felt chilled. His insistence about the money was disturbing. Those who knew of her work also knew that she did it on a voluntary basis. Even though she needed the money from her gallery contracts, she never intended to accept payment for her mentoring. She couldn't profit from a child in trouble. And if Jake McKenzie was who he said he was, he should know that.

"ANDREA, we're almost there." Jake glanced over at his daughter. But she didn't respond, instead staring out the window.

He pictured the bright, happy child she had been before her mother's defection. Laughter had come to her easily then. And she would have been chattering nonstop during the ride. Today she hadn't spoken half a dozen words since they'd gotten in the car. His heart ached for what she had lost, what she continued to lose.

It was nearly six o'clock. He had wanted to return to the Hill Country earlier, but Andrea had been particularly uncooperative. Since Brynn Alder had seemed spooked at midday, he didn't want to escalate her uneasiness by showing up after dark. He knew he had a fight on his hands to get the woman to reverse her decision. One that more phone calls wouldn't win. But surely when she looked into Andrea's face, saw the drugged emptiness of her eyes, the pain even massive medication couldn't mask…

Spotting Brynn's house, he turned in. As he parked, a huge dog bounded toward the car. Recognizing the lively setter from earlier, he got out of the car, then opened the passenger door. Andrea stepped out and the dog jumped up on her, its paws on her shoulders.

She was paralyzed for a moment, looking scared. However, the dog began licking her face and the fright receded.

As Jake watched, stunned to see Andrea respond to anything, they were suddenly surrounded by the three other dogs. Looking up, Jake saw Brynn Alder run around the side of her house. When she spotted him, she stopped. To his surprise, he saw fear in her face.

Exasperation he could understand. But not fear. Then it hit him. If she was here alone, she probably felt vulnerable.

He lifted a hand in greeting. She didn't look reassured. Her gaze shifted, taking in Andrea and the dog.

"Shamus, down!" she commanded.

The dog licked Andrea's face one last time, then obeyed.

Brynn approached, signaling her dogs, three of which trotted to her side. "Mr. McKenzie. What are you doing here?"

"I brought my daughter to meet you."

Shamus stayed at the girl's side as she turned. Brynn felt a stab in her heart. Although the girl's face didn't resemble her daughter's, in hindsight the pain she saw there was familiar. Even though it had only surfaced on occasion, it must have been the pain that had eventually caused Sarah to take her own life.

Brynn gulped back her emotion as Jake McKenzie stared curiously at her. She took a few steps forward, unable to resist the lure of the child. Oh, to have a chance again with Sarah, to make right what she hadn't done when Sarah was alive. To save her this time…

"Mrs. Alder?"

Brynn jerked her gaze from the girl to Jake McKenzie.

"This is Andrea."

Brynn curved her trembling lips into a smile. "It's good to meet you, Andrea."

The girl didn't respond.

Brynn wasn't bothered by the lack of reaction.

Instead she said, "Let's go inside. You're probably thirsty after your long drive."

Jake looked relieved to hear the invitation. Dropping an arm over Andrea's shoulders, he gently shepherded her inside, walking into the comfortable room. Once they'd sat down, Shamus settled at Andrea's feet. McKenzie watched his daughter. "He likes you, Annie."

Hesitantly she reached out to pet the dog. In return, the gentle giant gazed adoringly at her.

Brynn reluctantly pulled her own gaze away. "Make yourselves comfortable. I'll get some iced tea." She left the hall, Virgil at her heels.

When she returned a few minutes later, with the tea, Andrea was still stroking the dog.

"Shamus usually won't settle down for more than two minutes." Brynn placed the tray on the round coffee table, trying to keep her hands from shaking. "He must like you, Andrea."

The child looked up at Brynn with such pain-filled eyes it tore again at her heart. Jake McKenzie hadn't exaggerated.

"He's nice," Andrea said finally, her voice soft.

Brynn continued studying the child. "Yes, he is. Do you like dogs?"

Andrea shrugged.

It wasn't an eloquent response, but Brynn recognized a slim crack in her apathy. She remembered how Sarah had used the same gesture when words just wouldn't do or were difficult to summon.

Andrea reminded her so much of Sarah, who'd been so shaken by what life had dealt her. As she had hundreds of times since, Brynn wondered how differently things might have turned out if she'd been more aware then.

But her earlier suspicions couldn't be ignored. What if the child was simply a terribly effective prop McKenzie was using?

Brynn turned to him. "Sweet tea or plain?"

"Plain, thanks."

She handed him a glass. "And you, Andrea?"

"Sweet, I guess."

As she poured the tea, Brynn studied the girl, wanting to connect with her. "What do you like best about school?"

Andrea didn't look up from the dog. "Nothing."

Jake caught Brynn's gaze, his expression pointedly reminding her of his earlier words.

She placed Andrea's glass on the table. But the girl didn't reach for the tea. Like her dull eyes, the vacant expression could be the result of drugs. Her skin was unnaturally pale, her eyes shadowed with dark circles. Brynn looked from the girl to Jake McKenzie. There was a definite resemblance, especially in their hair coloring. More telling, every time Jake's glance fell on his daughter, it filled with genuine concern. His love for Andrea was a nearly palpable thing stretching between the wounded pair. Apparently he was who he said he was. And his daughter clearly needed help. She looked fragile enough to break.

Brynn remembered Jake's dire prediction— that Andrea was running out of time. What if he was right? Could she turn her back on the girl and risk the worst? Despite her fatigue, Brynn knew the answer. She wouldn't, couldn't allow that to happen.

The old, weathered grandfather clock chimed, reminding Brynn of the time. "Andrea, would you take Shamus outside, please?"

The girl hesitated, her hand still on the dog. She glanced up at her father, who nodded. "I guess so."

Brynn pointed to the terrace doors. "You can go that way. The other dogs may follow."

Andrea and Shamus walked outside. The two

terriers trailed them, but the Border collie remained at Brynn's side.

As soon as Andrea was out of hearing, Jake leaned forward, urgency etched in his features. "Well?"

"I can see that Andrea needs help."

"*Your* help."

"Andrea's case is different from the children I've dealt with so far. I've had no professional training, other than psychology classes in college. Giving children time away from their day-to-day lives, from the stress even well-meaning parents can put on their children, is how I help. But in Andrea's case…" Brynn paused, swallowing back the memories pushing at her. "Are you certain the relationship with her mother is beyond repair?"

He frowned. "My ex-wife only agreed to have Andrea in return for marriage and a guaranteed financial arrangement. But she'd had all she could take—her words, not mine. When she filed for divorce, she wanted more money, but nothing to do with Andrea." He stood suddenly and turned toward the windows. "I never guessed a woman could have absolutely no maternal feelings. But Val thought she'd wasted enough time, said she hadn't signed up for a life sentence. I felt Andrea was better off with no mother than one who resented her. Forcing Val into motherhood was doing no favors for Andrea. I always thought Val would come to love her. How could she not?'' Shaking his head, he pivoted back toward Brynn. ''This conversation isn't helping Andrea.''

''If I'm going to help her, I'll need to know everything.''

Light flashed in his eyes. ''You're going to take on Andrea's case?''

''I'll let you know by Monday. My circumstances haven't changed, but I'll try to work around them.''

''I'm still prepared to pay you more than—''

''No. As I told you, I do not, will not, accept money for helping a child.''

He stared at her curiously. With just one question, she had managed to pry more from him than he had confided to anyone else in years. And although he'd received a sterling recommendation regarding Brynn, he wished he knew more. Her personal life was a mystery.

Brynn glanced toward the terrace. ''In the event that I'm able to work with Andrea, let's take care of a few preliminaries. While you make out your contact list, I'll write a list of suggested things for Andrea to pack. She's free to bring along some personal items as well, but I ask that you eliminate anything noisy, such as CDs. The quiet here forces discussion.''

There was a time when Andrea could laugh and talk over anything, no matter how loud or distracting. Back then, on his return from work-related travel, it was as though his daughter had saved up everything that had happened while he was gone, filling him in on each detail. Val hadn't cared. She was glad when he was away, discontented when he was home. But not his Annie.

Now, though, it worried him to travel. Every time he returned, it seemed he'd lost another piece of his daughter. Thin and pale, she looked as though she'd gone through a long illness. It was emotional, not physiological, but the result was the same. Andrea was fading away. "We'll comply with your rules."

Brynn studied him. "I hope you mean that."

He drew his eyebrows together. "You doubt it?"

"My methods aren't completely conventional. Each child dictates his or her treatment."

"As long as it doesn't hurt Andrea, I'm on board."

"Good." Brynn paused. "Because my priority will be Andrea."

"That's what I would expect."

"I hope you mean that."

"One hundred percent." Jake studied her, wondering what prompted this woman to sacrifice so much of her time. He also wanted to know about the other members of the household before entrusting his daughter to Brynn. "Your husband must be a very understanding man."

"My husband is dead." Brynn's voice was matter-of-fact, but her eyes betrayed her pain.

"You live here alone?"

Wariness stiffened her expression and stance. She reached for her dog's collar. "Not completely."

Unwilling to frighten or put her off even more, Jake didn't persist. There would be plenty of time to ask his other questions, *if* she accepted Andrea.

CHAPTER TWO

AFTER A SLEEPLESS NIGHT, Brynn phoned the Cranstons early the next morning to check on Jake McKenzie's story. Unable to reach them, she left a message. Although young Andrea had touched her deeply, Brynn couldn't ignore the possible danger. Having moved twice in the past year, she also couldn't compromise this last safe place she'd come to call home.

Brynn thought of the moves that had brought her here. First from the home she'd shared with Kirk, then from the last home she'd shared with her daughter.

She stood, pacing as she remembered Kirk's car accident, the call telling her that he was dead. Then that terrible numbness.

Her valiant daughter had stood beside her as they'd buried him, both unable to believe he was really gone. On their return home they'd discovered that the house had been broken into. The police told Brynn there were criminals who read the obituaries, then used the gruesome opportunity to burgle the deceased's home. But nothing of much value other than Kirk's cameras had been stolen.

Brynn had also begun receiving many hang-up calls. But then, she'd been solicited for everything from cemetery plots to cruises after Kirk's death. However, after one of the calls, she realized someone had been in the house again while she and Sarah were out. It was more subtle that second time, but she saw the signs.

The police took her concerns seriously, but they questioned whether Kirk could have been involved in something unsavory. Although Brynn had vehemently denied that suggestion, she had agreed to allow them to search her home, and later, Kirk's studio.

Not finding anything, the police also examined Kirk's photos, which had been placed in storage. Detectives spent a good deal of time examining the collection, but could see no connection between the pictures and the break-in. There seemed to be no clandestine or accidental shot that would compel someone to try to steal the evidence.

Worried about her daughter's safety, Brynn had moved to a new neighborhood, hoping that whatever the intruders wanted would be forgotten once she and Sarah disappeared.

But then Sarah had died, a tragic incident that had all but shattered Brynn's own interest in life. There'd been another break-in, but she hadn't cared. Her family and friends had, however. At Julia's insistence, she'd moved to the ranch. And now she needed to learn as much as she could about the McKenzies.

Andrea's school wouldn't divulge any information. Brynn could certainly understand why, but it didn't get her any closer to establishing McKenzie's credibility.

A call to his employer was equally disappointing. They had a strict policy. Nothing could be revealed unless requested in writing, accompanied by the employee's signed release.

Frustrated, Brynn phoned her friend and confidante, Julia, outlining the situation.

Julia was immediately protective. "I'm not sure I like the sound of this. It could be perfectly innocent, but then again… Listen, why don't I come out? Stay the weekend? I have some mail for you."

Brynn didn't hesitate; the prospect of an ally was immensely comforting. "That would be great if you really don't have any plans."

Julia sighed with mock drama. "Zip. I'd have better luck meeting the right man in the middle of the Sahara."

Brynn chuckled unexpectedly. No matter how down she felt, Julia had a way of making her smile. "Jules, you turn down more men than most women ever meet."

"I'm glad you're convinced one of these frogs will turn out to be Prince Charming. I've stopped believing he exists."

Brynn had a sudden image of her late husband, the man she had planned to spend her life with, her prince in every way that counted.

"Brynn, sorry. I didn't think—"

"No, no!" she said dismissively. "You're right. I did my fair share of 'dissecting' frogs until I met Kirk." She pushed back the thick hair that fell across her forehead. "And you can't keep monitoring every word when you talk to me. Some things will always remind me of Kirk…and Sarah. And that's not always bad, you know."

"Yeah, I know," Julia replied in a gentle

tone. "I'm going to grab a few things and get rolling. Anything you need from civilization?"

Everything and nothing. Sometimes it was difficult to believe that she'd once lived only a few miles from the heart of the city. "Just your company."

"You got it, kid. I'll make a few quick stops and then I'll be on my way."

Brynn hung up, already feeling better. It helped to have someone to share her concerns with. Always independent, she had tried to remain so during her marriage, but it had been easy to become accustomed to having someone to lean on, to talk things over with. So much had changed with Kirk's death.

Virgil pushed his muzzle into her hand and she petted her loyal friend. "We're going to have company, Virg. Julia's coming."

The dog wagged his tail, recognizing Julia's name. Before she'd lost her husband and daughter, Brynn's life had been filled with friends and family. Although her father had passed away and she had no siblings, Brynn had never felt short of family. She was close to her mother and had an array of aunts, uncles and cousins. Although they got together more rarely as she and her cousins had started families of their own, they were a supportive bunch. But when her life was threatened, Brynn hadn't wanted to expose the people she cared about to danger. Most of her friends and family accepted her wish to be left alone.

Julia, however, had refused to be shut out. Her offer had proved to be a godsend, enabling Brynn to assure her mother that she would be safe. Now she and her mother talked a few times a week. Their phone calls, along with Julia's visits, kept her connected.

Feeling a little less worried, Brynn freshened up Julia's bedroom and then headed to her studio. Once absorbed in her work, she didn't notice that the hours passed, until a clatter at the back door startled her. Her heart pounded as the dogs barked. It took her a few moments to recognize that their noise wasn't a warning. Brynn placed a hand to her chest, trying to steady her irregular breathing. Then, realizing it must be Julia, she grabbed a towel, hurriedly wiping off her hands as she dashed toward the back door.

Surrounded by adoring animals, including her own dog, Lobo, Julia lifted a hand in greeting. "It's hard to believe I started this menagerie."

Virgil waited patiently for his pat and Julia didn't disappoint him. "You're keeping Brynn safe, aren't you, boy?"

"My shadow," Brynn agreed, stepping through the exuberant mass of dogs to hug her friend. "It's good to see you. Thanks for coming."

"It's a great excuse to get me out of the madness. I start winding down about fifty miles outside the city. I forget how stressed I am until some of it eases."

"That's why this is a good place to escape, for both of us." Brynn's smile widened. "But you'd be bored beyond belief if you lived here."

Julia sighed. "I suppose so. I'm used to getting whatever I want whenever I want. Speaking of which, I brought goodies!"

Even the dogs looked intrigued when Brynn and Julia reached the car. The back of the SUV was open and Julia picked up an overflowing box. "Everything we need for a weekend in the country, city-style!"

Brynn reached for the carton. "Let me help."

Handing it to her, Julia picked up a cooler. "Okay. This needs to go in the fridge."

They opened the box and cooler in the

kitchen. The goodies included bottles of Brynn's favorite wine, Godiva chocolates, Häagen-Dazs ice cream and an assortment of treats from the most exclusive deli in San Antonio.

"I nearly forgot the best thing!"

Brynn groaned. "You don't think we can possibly eat more than this?"

Julia unearthed one more package and held it up like a trophy. "Shipley's doughnuts!"

"The world's best," Brynn agreed, lifting the lid to eye the contents almost reverently. "We'll have to walk twenty miles to burn these off."

"I'm game."

Brynn filched a chocolate-filled doughnut. "Me, too."

"I brought milk, but we can have coffee if you want."

Looking at the empty pot, Brynn frowned. "I meant to make some, but—"

"You got caught up in your work. Good." Julia's smile was knowing and kind. "It's been too long since you've been able to do that."

After she'd lost her family, potting had been both a blessing and a curse. At times Brynn couldn't get past mixing fresh clay. Inspiration seemed beyond her. Instead it was as though she fought a fog that distorted her artistic vision. Yet at other times, pottery was the only thing that took her out of the endless cycle of self-blame and pain. When she awoke each day, she never knew whether she'd be able to work or not.

Julia measured out the coffee. "While this brews, I'll bring in the other coolers. I thought the freezer might need filling."

In order to keep a low profile, Brynn rarely ventured into the small nearby town of Walburg. Instead, the huge walk-in freezer was well stocked. The butler's pantry and commercial freezer had been installed by Julia's grandfather, whose hunting trips often ran into weeks or months. And Julia's father had continued the tradition. Although some of the equipment had been updated, including the addition of a commercial refrigerator, they served the same purpose. A person could remain at the ranch house for months without venturing out for supplies.

As they unloaded the coolers, Brynn felt her throat catch. Julia had done so much for her.

Her friend panted as she pushed a box of steaks onto the top shelf of the freezer. "Whew!" She rubbed cold hands together, then glanced up at Brynn, her face sobering. "What is it?"

Brynn swallowed the rush of emotion. "Wondering where I'd be if you hadn't stepped in with your offer. Your haven has become mine."

Julia took her arm. "It can't be said enough—that's what friends are for. Brynn, you've always been there for me when I've slipped, fallen or just plain skidded. I'm glad the house is here—that it's safe. Come on, let's dig into those doughnuts and you can tell me more about this guy who's trying to push his daughter on you."

Somehow it didn't seem that sinister in the light of Julia's practical optimism. Still, over doughnuts and fresh coffee, Brynn told all she knew about Jake McKenzie.

"Have the Cranstons called you back?"

Brynn frowned. "No. And that's the biggest hitch. They were so grateful that I helped Susan I can't understand why they would disregard my wishes."

"Just guessing, I'd say if they did tell McKenzie about you, they didn't realize the seriousness of compromising your privacy."

Reluctantly, Brynn nodded. "I suppose you're right."

Julia added cream to her coffee. "And I can't help wondering how McKenzie came up with Susan's name if he's not the real deal."

"Good point." Brynn abandoned her doughnut. "Unless I'm being watched."

"Maybe we shouldn't take that leap quite so fast."

"I'll try the Cranstons again." Brynn paused. "Or maybe it would be best to speak with their doctor first."

Leaving the table, she put in a call to the psychiatrist who had referred the Cranstons. He was with a patient, but the receptionist assured Brynn she would pass along the message.

"So we still know nothing for sure," Julia concluded as Brynn clicked off the phone.

"Yep."

"Brynn, what *aren't* you telling me?"

She closed her eyes briefly, the words difficult to summon. "The girl, McKenzie's daughter. Her pain…I recognized it. Even though I didn't realize it at the time, I see now that it's like Sarah's was. I can't help thinking this could be a second chance for me."

"You sure that's not wishful thinking?" Julia asked gently.

"I suppose it sounds that way." Brynn exhaled. "And I can see how it appears from your perspective. Doesn't seem credible, does it?"

Julia's mouth lifted in a wry half smile. "I'm not making any judgments. I haven't walked in your shoes."

Familiar pain filled her. "Don't."

Julia linked her arm with Brynn's. "How 'bout getting a start on those twenty miles?"

Taking a healing stroll through the soothing countryside sounded like a very good idea. She pocketed the cell phone. "Just what the doctor ordered."

Julia grabbed another doughnut with her free hand. "We might have to make that thirty miles."

BY SUNDAY EVENING, Brynn knew little more than she had before Julia arrived. Her friend provided a stabilizing, calming effect. But Brynn needed to know more about Jake McKenzie, especially since his daughter remained in her thoughts.

Sipping a glass of pleasingly tart blush wine, Brynn stared at the phone, willing it to ring.

"The Cranstons might have gone out of town for the weekend," Julia suggested.

"I thought of that. But it irks me that the doctor hasn't phoned."

"A doctor on the weekend? You'd have a better chance of getting through to the White House."

"So what do I tell McKenzie tomorrow?"

Julia met her gaze. "I didn't meet him, so I can't give an opinion. But my gut instinct says protect this place."

"Hmm."

"It's more than just McKenzie, isn't it?"

Brynn placed her glass on the table, restlessness overtaking her. "I can't run forever, especially since I don't know what I'm running from."

"The unknown's damn scary," Julia advised gently. "But if the police couldn't discover a motive for the break-ins, how can you expect to? You know they scanned Kirk's photos, compared them with the national data bank. And they admitted the photos were exactly what they appeared to be. No covert snap of anyone famous or infamous."

"The second set of detectives believed that was because photography was supposed to be Kirk's *cover*." Even now, the bile rose in her throat as she remembered their insinuations. They felt he must have been involved in something shady and ultimately lethal.

"But you know the truth."

Did she? In her darkest moments, Brynn wondered if she could have somehow been wrong— horribly, terribly wrong. The man she knew had loved his family and put them first. Yet she had no explanation for what had happened after his death. "I'm probably overreacting."

"You have to be concerned about your safety, not only for yourself but for your work. Think of the children you've already had here. Where would they be without your help?"

As true as that might be, Brynn also knew that she couldn't live with herself if, out of fear, she turned Andrea McKenzie away and the child took her own life.

The phone rang. It was Dr. Halliwell, the psychiatrist who had referred Susan Cranston. He admitted that he'd passed Brynn's number along to Jake McKenzie. The men had been roommates in college. And he'd also thought it helpful for Jake to speak with the Cranstons, because Susan's experience had been so positive. Since the doctor had only Brynn's cell number to pass along, there was nothing to reproach the man for. He didn't know about Brynn's special circumstances.

After he hung up, Brynn related his end of the conversation to Julia. "And I suppose the Cranstons saw no harm in giving out my location to their doctor's friend." Deflated by the rush of conflicting emotions, Brynn collapsed in one of the comfortable chairs. "Do you think the threat could possibly be past?"

Julia's eyes filled with worry. "How can you know for sure without exposing yourself?"

"You're right. And I don't think I could face another move—even if I had a place to run to."

CHAPTER THREE

SOMETHING HAD CHANGED in Brynn Alder. Jake didn't know why, but he wasn't questioning their good fortune.

True to her word, Brynn had called him first thing that morning. Without hesitation, she had agreed to start working with Andrea. And she'd willingly answered all his queries, leading him to believe his daughter would be safe with her.

In return, he had complied with Brynn's wish to speak to the psychiatrist about easing Andrea off her medications.

Jake then wasted no time collecting Andrea and her belongings. Now, turning in at the unmarked road that led to Brynn's house, he squeezed Annie's hand, offering reassurance. But she didn't respond. God, he wished he could repair all the damage his ex-wife had inflicted.

He'd been an idiot to become involved with a woman who cared for nothing but herself. And naive to believe that motherhood would some-how change that. Still, Val's presence had meant a great deal to Annie, since he was gone so fre-quently.

He was as riddled with guilt as with worry. His career had provided all the material benefits his family needed. And since he was dissatisfied with his marriage, it had also provided an es-cape. But there hadn't been one for Annie.

Jake glanced over at her. "We're almost there."

No response.

He withheld a sigh as the ranch came into sight. It sat on sloping land at the base of a shel-tering hill. The stone house looked as though it could stand for many more generations.

Driving into the wide yard, he parked beneath one of the many shade trees. As he got out of the car, the front door opened and Brynn ap-peared. Apparently she had been watching for them.

She waited beside a glider on the porch, her face partially hidden by flower-filled hanging baskets, though he caught a quick impression of her tall, slim form and long golden hair. As be-fore, the Border collie stood by her side.

Picking up a suitcase and taking his daughter's hand, he climbed the wide steps to the porch. Jake couldn't help feeling as though he and Andrea were new kids on the first day of school.

Brynn stepped closer, gesturing to the entryway. "Andrea, your room is at the top of the stairs, first door on the left."

Jake gripped the large suitcase more tightly, glancing at the backpack hanging from his daughter's other hand. When Brynn offered to help her get settled in, Andrea stepped back, and Jake sensed her distress. "I can carry the suitcase upstairs, get her unpacked."

"That will be fine. I made some sandwiches and lemonade. I'll carry them out to the terrace."

Grateful for her sensitivity, Jake climbed the stairs with his daughter. The room Brynn had chosen for Andrea was both soothing and cheerful. Freshly picked sunflowers and other wildflowers he couldn't identify were arranged in vases around the room, providing bursts of color. Sage-green walls framed the wide, tall window.

Andrea listlessly accepted his help, not caring where her belongings were put. She dragged her feet as they walked downstairs. Even though he knew this stay was for her benefit, Jake couldn't repress his guilt, sensing her confusion and fright.

"Annie, Mrs. Alder's going to help you. And I'm only a phone call away."

She didn't look reassured.

His heart heavy, Jake draped one arm over Andrea's shoulders as they walked out to the cobbled terrace.

Brynn waited for them at a redwood table also decorated with sunflowers. As they approached, she poured the lemonade. "I'm always parched after a long drive."

"Looks good," Jake agreed, accepting a glass.

Andrea ignored the cool drink as Shamus settled beside her. Hesitantly, the girl petted his shaggy head. Remembering how she'd responded to the dog on her first visit, Brynn was encouraged. Often animals could reach children when no human could.

Once they'd eaten, Brynn took them on a tour of the house and immediate grounds. Inside the hazy, sunlight-pricked interior of the barn, bales of clean hay were stacked in a stair-step fashion, and a small tack room smelled of aged leather. Six horses were stabled in generous stalls. The

Fords had always loved riding on the land they owned.

Julia was the last of her family, and the ranch was important to her. Even though these days she didn't live on the old homestead, Brynn was certain her friend would never sell the property. It meant too much to her.

Walking farther into the barn, Brynn spotted Roy Bainter, a local man who had cared for the Fords' horses for decades. He and his wife, Mary, lived close to town. To date, Roy was the only local she'd met. Brynn had found that he was kind but taciturn, with a soft spot for kids.

"Hello, Roy. I'd like you to meet some new friends."

The older man removed his hand from the mane of the horse he was grooming. The animals loved Roy, and the horse nudged his shoulder with her muzzle.

Jake chuckled. "Looks like we're making the filly jealous."

Roy met Jake's gaze with an appraising one of his own. "You know horses?"

Jake nodded. "I took lessons, then rode regularly at a stable in the city. But that was a lot of years ago."

"Mebbe. But a man doesn't forget the things that count."

The men shook hands.

Brynn continued the introductions. "And this is Jake's daughter, Andrea."

Roy glanced down at the girl, who didn't speak. "Good, a quiet one. She'll do."

Andrea's eyes showed a glimmer of surprise.

"You know anything about horses, girl?"

Brynn didn't think she would answer. But then Andrea slowly shook her head.

"Well, you're young enough to learn. This here's Lizzie. Most of the time she's a good old girl. Now and then she thinks she's the queen of England and I gotta call her Elizabeth." Roy glanced up at Brynn. "Mary baked an extra pie. I put it in the kitchen."

She hadn't noticed either the pie or his entry, Brynn realized. But it was the custom of the area, and doors weren't kept locked. She'd tried to take Julia's advice and not panic at the innocent gestures. "Thank you, Roy. We'll enjoy it."

Seeing that Andrea was intrigued with the horses and not paying attention to her father, Brynn touched Jake's arm, gesturing toward the wide, open double doors.

Jake accompanied her outside. But he looked back, his gaze lingering on Andrea, his expression troubled.

Watching him, Brynn understood the unspoken emotion. Although he'd fought to bring Andrea here, he hated leaving her. "Once Andrea and I become more acquainted, I think we'll get on well." She smiled gently, hoping he could take reassurance from the words.

"I'm sure you will." He shifted his glance from his daughter. "I'm going to stay in Walburg for a few days, to be close by."

Brynn frowned.

"What is it?"

"I don't know much about Walburg, but I doubt there's a motel."

He looked at her curiously. How could she live in this remote area and not know much about the closest town? "I'll find something. Now I'd better say goodbye to Andrea."

Retracing his steps, he approached his daughter and took her hand. "Remember, Annie, Mrs. Alder is going to help you."

He nearly lost his resolve when a tear escaped her eye. Instead, he bent down for a final but fierce hug.

"I'll phone," he promised after releasing Andrea. "And you have my cell number."

Roy turned away, busying himself with the horse feed.

Realizing Andrea wasn't going to reply, Jake forced himself not to look back as he left the barn.

Brynn stood beside the corral. "I know you're worried about her. I would hate to leave a troubled child of my own with a stranger."

Jake searched her face, hoping he'd made the right decision, that he was wise to place his trust in this woman.

Her kind smile seemed to say that she understood his concerns, that it would be all right.

Even though she shut the gate quietly after he passed through it, the closing sounded so final. Realizing that lingering wouldn't help Andrea, he climbed into his SUV and drove back to the main road.

Once he reached Walburg, it didn't take long to drive its meager streets. He spotted a church, a school, various stores and small businesses, an old-fashioned hamburger place and even an additional small eatery. But he didn't see a motel or inn.

He stopped at the gas station and began pumping fuel. Jake didn't see anyone until the he'd replaced the pump, his tank full. A man dressed in neat but well-used overalls emerged from the garage. Jake handed over his credit card. "Is there a motel or boardinghouse nearby?"

"The closest is probably in Kalochton. Not much of a place, but it'd do in a pinch."

"How far is Kalochton?"

"About fifty miles."

An hour's drive. He wanted to be closer. "And if it's full, how far is another one?"

"Another fifty miles. But the place in Kalochton's never full except during Octoberfest."

Jake accepted his receipt. "Thanks for the information."

"Thanks for your business. Stop by again if you're in town."

The unexpected small-town courtesy reminded Jake of days past, when hospitality had been the trademark of small businesses. A time before one-stop superstores had changed rural America. "I'll do that."

Encouraged by the man's friendliness, Jake considered it a good sign that Andrea would be close to this community.

Traveling on the two-lane road, he found it took an hour and a half to reach Kalochton. All that could be said for the motel was that his room had an adequate bed—although it had to be pulled out from the wall. And once down, the Murphy bed filled the room. There was no desk on which to spread out the contents of his packed briefcase, and between a very spare shower stall and a small sink, the minuscule bathroom had just enough space to turn around in.

Unconcerned about the accommodations, Jake phoned the ranch. Mrs. Alder answered, saying there was nothing to report. She didn't attempt to falsely assure him that all was well. They both knew Andrea was far from well.

Although exhausted by the emotional upheaval, Jake knew he couldn't nap during the day; his restless energy never allowed it. He was accustomed to staying in hotels around the world, where his work always absorbed him. But now, even after he'd unrolled a set of plans, he couldn't concentrate. All he could see was his daughter's tortured face, the pull of her pleading eyes. And the woman who might well be Annie's last chance.

BRYNN RUBBED HER FOREHEAD, trying to fend off the beginnings of a headache. It had been a long day, this first one with Andrea. That wasn't uncommon. Most young teens initially resented being sent to her. Andrea, however, didn't display resentment, but rather hopelessness. And that, Brynn knew, was far more difficult to overcome.

She'd had one small victory. Convincing Andrea to drink a fortified milkshake wasn't a huge accomplishment, but the steps to recovery were often small.

Now, Andrea had gone to bed. She was docile about accepting the rules. But the apathy was hard to take. Brynn glanced at her watch. Enough time had passed that Andrea should be asleep.

Walking quietly, Brynn entered the guest room, accompanied by the quiet clicking of Virgil's toenails. The small night-light she always left on glowed in the still room. Shamus, who had stuck close to Andrea all day, was stretched out beside the bed.

Stepping around the dog, Brynn studied the girl. Even in sleep, she looked agitated. Brynn gently stroked back the hair that fell over Andrea's cheek, remembering how she had often done the same to her daughter. It was one of the many things she missed. In twelve years of tucking Sarah in, no day had been complete without that ritual.

Sighing, she stepped back, stooping to pat Shamus, then went out quietly, leaving the door ajar so she could hear Andrea if there was a problem in the night.

Once back in her own room, Brynn strolled to the window. Outside, the sky was clear and dark, unmarred by city lights. The quiet, the peace…it had helped her these past months. But the nights were still bad—the loneliness of her bed, the lack of someone with whom to talk over all the big or little events of the day.

Her cats, Bert and Ernie, were curled up on the pillow next to hers. The terriers, Molly and Duncan, were stretched out on the thick rug beside the bed. But Virgil wouldn't rest until she did. After climbing into bed, Brynn picked up the book on her nightstand. But her mind traveled from the page to the child down the hall. After an hour, she gave up trying to read and turned off the light. Sleep was usually elusive, but she hoped it would come tonight.

Some time later, in that blurry state before being truly asleep, Brynn jerked awake when she heard a piercing scream. Heart racing, she touched her lips, wondering if the scream had come from her own mouth, as it had so often in the past, the product of her continuing nightmares.

But the wail continued. Jumping from her bed, Brynn tore down the hall and into Andrea's room. The child's eyes were still closed, her body rigid, held in the grip of a nightmare.

Sitting on the edge of the bed, Brynn gently grasped the girl's shoulders. "Andrea, wake up, sweetie. Come on. Wake up."

Andrea's eyes opened and she flinched. A rapid pulse was visible in her thin throat. Patting her back, Brynn spoke motherly, comforting words, but Andrea didn't respond. Terror convulsed her, then huge, wrenching sobs erupted.

"Andrea, it's all right. It was a nightmare. Scary, I know, but not real."

Andrea shook her head in denial. "It's real! I'm here!" Through the words, she gasped for breath.

It hit Brynn what she meant. Apparently feeling abandoned by her father, Andrea thought the nightmare *was* her life. Brynn couldn't let the child believe her father would desert her as her mother had. "Annie, do you want me to call your dad?"

The girl's quivering head finally bobbed up and down.

"I'll go phone. Shamus and Virgil will stay with you." Directing Virgil to stay, Brynn hurried downstairs to locate Jake's number. She didn't want to explain the nightmare in front of Andrea, yet she worried about leaving her alone for long. Luckily, Jake grasped the situation quickly and agreed to come at once.

Back upstairs, Brynn did her best to comfort Andrea, but the girl's sobbing continued. Brynn knew how it felt to have her heart broken. But it was worse, far worse, seeing it happen to a child.

CHAPTER FOUR

THE BEDROOM WAS QUIET when Jake entered. Andrea was curled in the fetal position, her face red and puffy. The dog that had taken a liking to his daughter stood beside the bed, watching him carefully.

As Jake sat down on the edge of the bed, the mattress dipped under his weight, alerting Andrea. As soon as she saw him, she broke into tears, the sobs wrenching her thin body.

Instinctively he drew her close to his chest. "Annie, it's me. You're safe now."

But her sobbing continued.

"I told you I was only a phone call away."

She pulled back, staring at him doubtfully.

Jake searched her eyes, remembering Brynn's words. *She thinks you've abandoned her.* Could Brynn be right? Did Andrea really believe that? "Annie, you're here *only* because you need help that I don't know how to give."

"Will you stay with me?" she pleaded.

"Why don't I sit with you until you fall asleep?"

Her eyes clouded and Jake wondered what he'd said that was wrong. Since Val had left it seemed nothing he did was right. After several minutes passed, he patted her shoulder. "I need to talk to Mrs. Alder, then I'll be right back."

He could hear Andrea's continued sniffling as he left the room and headed downstairs to the den. Wordlessly, Brynn handed him a mug of steaming coffee.

"Thanks," he murmured gratefully.

"I thought you might need it. How's Andrea?"

"A little better. I told her I'd stay with her until she falls asleep. Actually, I'd like to stay with her the night. Will that wreak havoc with your house rules?"

"No. Andrea needs you tonight."

"Thank you, Mrs. Al—"

"Call me Brynn, please. You'll find an extra blanket in the bedroom closet."

"That's kind of you."

"It's going to take time with Andrea, Mr.—"

"Jake," he interrupted.

"Jake," she repeated, her soft voice giving

his name a lilt he'd never heard before. "But, however long it takes, I won't give up on her."

Gratified, Jake nodded. "I'd better get back to Andrea."

"I'll leave the lights on in the den, and if you need me, my room is at the end of the upstairs hall."

Once back in Andrea's room, he moved the desk chair next to the bed. She watched him, her eyes anxious.

"Try to sleep, Annie."

"You won't leave, Daddy?"

His heart clenched. It had been a long time since she'd called him "Daddy." He thought that had gone the way of Santa Claus and the tooth fairy. "No, I won't leave." *At least not tonight.* Surely her reaction was simply first-night jitters.

Watching as Annie's eyes began to droop, he hoped Brynn had a touch of magic in her arsenal.

AFTER A NEARLY SLEEPLESS night, Brynn gave up the battle and rose early, deciding they would all need a substantial breakfast. She'd checked on Andrea twice during the night. Both times she was asleep, but her father wasn't. It didn't look as though Jake had moved. He'd lifted his gaze long enough to acknowledge Brynn's presence each time, but neither of them had spoken, not wanting to waken Andrea.

Reaching the kitchen, Brynn opened the door for the dogs. All of them, except Shamus, who hadn't left Andrea's room, loped outside. Ignoring the frisky animals, Bert and Ernie strolled behind them, delicately stretching until the path was clear.

Measuring the coffee, Brynn decided to make it strong. For a moment she stared out through the kitchen window, thinking of her daughter. Why hadn't she seen the symptoms? So caught up in her grief over Kirk, had she simply not seen what was right in front of her?

Remembering how Sarah had loved French toast, Brynn whisked the egg mixture, hoping it might appeal to Andrea, too. Although she hadn't seen Andrea when she was well, Brynn suspected that rather than going through an abrupt change, the child had slowly faded, emotionally and physically. Faded away until her state of mind was painfully obvious. Thinking again of Sarah, Brynn bit down on her bottom lip as a stray tear escaped. How could she have blinded herself to the most important thing in her life?

Hearing Jake clear his throat from across the room, she hastily swiped at the tear, composing her face. "Is Andrea awake?"

He looked at her curiously but didn't pry. "Yes. She's getting dressed. Coffee smells good."

Swallowing the lump in her throat, Brynn managed a small smile. "The mugs are in the cabinet on your right."

Pouring his own coffee, he glanced at the food she was preparing. "Looks good."

"After a rough night, I thought we could all use the reinforcement."

"I remember when Andrea used to consume a stack of pancakes, a bowl of cereal, and then be ready for more within an hour. These days…"

Hearing the wistful note in his voice, Brynn wanted to offer him some encouragement. "Yesterday she drank a milkshake. I'd added vitamin-infused protein powder, disguised by ice cream. I think it was a step in the right direction."

He looked at her gratefully. "Your reputation is well earned."

"There's still a long way to go, I'm afraid. A

lot of depressed kids lose their appetite. That's why I keep the protein powder and ice cream on hand. It's hard to resist a milkshake.''

''By the time I realized Andrea had a problem, I couldn't tempt her with anything.''

Brynn thought of her own failure to recognize Sarah's pain. ''Don't beat yourself up about it. You're doing something now.''

Nodding, he sipped the steaming coffee.

Brynn added cream to her own coffee. ''Let's see how today goes. After breakfast, I want to work with Andrea on my own.''

''I'll be at the motel in case...'' His words trailed off as Andrea silently entered the kitchen. Jake remembered the many times he'd pleaded for quiet when she'd bounded into a room, a flurry of movement and noise. ''Morning, Pooh.'' The old nickname slipped out, one he'd affectionately called her years before when she'd become obsessed with Winnie the Pooh.

She looked startled. ''Morning.'' The word was mumbled, but at least she'd replied. Shamus entered the kitchen with more noise than Andrea had.

''Would you let him out?'' Brynn asked.

''Okay.'' As Andrea did, the other dogs

rushed in, pushing past her to look for their own breakfast.

"I hope you like French toast," Brynn commented.

Andrea shrugged thin shoulders. "I'm not hungry."

"Then I'll only put a small portion on your plate."

Jake noticed Brynn hadn't put the food on a serving platter, instead arranging it on individual plates. Andrea didn't have to reach for anything, and the food was harder to ignore when placed right beneath her nose.

Flanked by adults, Andrea stared at her breakfast, then finally took a bite of the fragrant toast.

Jake glanced up, meeting Brynn's encouraging gaze. It was a small step, but he felt a bit of hope. And for today it was enough.

AFTER JAKE LEFT, Brynn worked to breach Andrea's apathy. First she assigned her a small chore, that of checking the pets' needs—their drinking water and sleeping quarters. The job was a simple one, but Brynn knew Andrea needed some responsibilities. And Shamus was by the girl's side again.

Brynn smiled at her. "Shamus has never

taken to anyone so quickly or completely before.''

Andrea gave her usual shrug, but couldn't conceal the spark of light in her gaze.

''Dogs are the best judges of people, you know.''

This time there was no shrug.

''I spoke to your doctor yesterday morning. With his approval, your dad and I agreed to begin easing off your meds.''

This time Brynn was certain she saw interest in Andrea's expression. ''Is Dad coming back tonight?''

''Why don't we see how it goes this evening?'' she suggested.

Andrea retreated again, until Shamus pushed his head against her arm. She hesitated, then petted the adoring animal. ''When do we start with my meds?''

''Tonight. How does that sound?''

She petted Shamus again. ''Okay.''

Studying her expression, Brynn saw the barely concealed desperation. But she wasn't going to fail this child. This child so like her own Sarah.

MINDFUL OF ANDREA'S fragile state, her susceptibility to a suicide attempt, Brynn had come to a difficult decision. That evening, she'd phoned Jake, asking him to bring an overnight bag. Now he paced the den as she outlined her suggestion that he stay at the ranch.

She saw the indecision on his face. "I've been trying to assess what she needs. And my instincts tell me that she needs you more than anything."

He paused. "I understand that."

"I'm not sure you do." Brynn leaned forward. "Jake, you and Andrea need to learn how to communicate all over again."

He frowned. "She's ill because her mother left."

"And because your relationship with her isn't filling the void."

Jake stiffened. "Admittedly, I travel a lot for my job—"

"That's no doubt part of it. But if you want this to work, you're going to have to be part of the relearning process."

Confused, he stared at her. "What exactly does that mean?"

"It means you need to be reeducated along with Andrea."

He wondered if she could be right. "Did you

ever wish you could do things over? Have a fresh start?''

Brynn's lips tightened. Instantly he remembered that her husband had died. ''God, I'm sorry,'' he exclaimed. ''I'm so focused on Andrea—''

''Completely understandable. There's nothing more important than our children.''

''And I won't be in your way?''

She shook her head.

He searched her eyes. ''As grateful as I am for what you're doing for Andrea, for both of us, I can't help but wonder—doesn't it intrude on your own life?''

''My life is simple,'' Brynn replied. ''And, yes, busy. I told you that when you first phoned.''

So she had. But what made this woman tick? Surely more than solitude and mentoring troubled children.

''Would you like some coffee?'' she offered.

''No thanks. I'm hoping for a good night's sleep.''

''In that case, why don't I show you to your room? I've put you in the one next to Andrea's.''

''Right.''

Once upstairs, Jake knocked quietly on Andrea's door, and his daughter jerked it open. Shamus stood by her side.

Her huge blue eyes widened. "Daddy? Is something wrong?"

"No. Good news, actually. Brynn has invited me to stay at the ranch while she works with you."

"Here?" In her eyes disbelief battled with hope. "Really?"

Jake smiled, the tenderness he felt for his child flooding him. "Really. In fact, I have the room next to yours."

Andrea glanced at him, then at Brynn. And the smallest smile pushed the corners of her mouth upward. "Starting now?"

He held up the overnight bag. "Yep. Tomorrow I'll go get the rest of my things and check out of the motel. Think you might sleep better now?"

Andrea nodded tremulously.

Brynn reached out, gently cupping Andrea's chin. "Your dreams should be filled with only good things now."

As though afraid the words themselves were a dream, Andrea glanced at her father for confirmation.

Brynn withdrew her hand. "'Night, Annie. Sleep well."

Jake watched as Brynn slipped into her room, noticing her quiet grace, her gentle manner.

Their new sleeping arrangements struck him as pretty cozy. But he was here for only one purpose. Regardless of how Brynn intrigued him.

CHAPTER FIVE

JAKE WATCHED A JACKRABBIT bound through the field, its loping gait like that of a miniature kangaroo. What an amazing bunch of creatures he'd seen in the previous week! It made sense that wildlife populated the sloping hills and deep arroyos. But back in the city it had never occurred to him that he'd actually see animals other than cats and dogs.

Jake hadn't owned a pet since he was a kid. The first years of his career had kept him too busy to care for one, and Val considered animals a messy nuisance. It was something he'd never challenged. Finding it easier to give in to Val's wishes and demands, he hadn't fought many issues. And luckily, despite Val's poor parenting, Andrea had been an easygoing, upbeat kid.

He remembered Brynn's words, not accusing, but disturbingly frank. She thought he was as much a part of the problem as Val's defection. Could she be right?

Jake wanted to believe he was close to his child, something he hadn't felt with his own father. His dad had never attended school events or Jake's football games.

Instead he had been obsessed with his career. And when he wasn't working, Harold McKenzie hadn't wanted to spend time with his son. Jake had never understood why his father had agreed to have a family at all. To this day there was a distance between them that had never been bridged.

Jake had always been adamant he wouldn't allow that kind of breakdown in his own family. And although his job involved travel, he had always made certain Andrea knew she was loved.

He shook his head wryly, wondering at the direction of his thoughts. It was the quiet here at the ranch, he decided. It gave him time to think of things he normally kept cataloged and bound.

When Jake had alerted the company that he was taking a leave of absence, rather than a working vacation, his second in command had jumped at the chance to take over. Yep, it was a world full of piranhas. But Jake didn't want his daughter to learn that lesson so young. She still deserved happy endings.

Hearing a quiet murmur of voices, he pushed forward through the knee-high grass in the meadow. His daughter and Brynn sat beneath a sturdy oak not far away, the dogs stretched out at their feet.

Even from a distance Jake could see some of the sweetness returning to his daughter's expression. Thank God she *had* an expression now. Some of the horrible blankness was fading.

His gaze shifted to Brynn, who was easy to watch. She wasn't a classic beauty, but Jake thought she was striking, even with her clear skin and large green eyes bare of makeup. He'd never understood the earth-muffin type. The women he knew spent more time on clothes and makeup than pets and wildflowers. And they didn't seek isolation.

He wondered if something had chased Brynn here. So far everything he'd learned about her checked out. Being a VP at Canyon had its benefits, including access to a top-notch security division.

The wind shifted and Virgil's head lifted. No doubt the watchful dog had caught his scent. Making more noise than necessary, Jake stamped through the meadow. Andrea casually glanced in his direction. Brynn, on the other hand, looked startled, her expression alert, watchful.

Again he wondered why.

She stood up. "I'm going to head back to the house and start dinner."

"Would you like some help?"

She shook her head. "Enjoy some time with Annie."

He glanced down at Andrea, pleased to see a touch of color in his daughter's face. He was about to comment on it when Brynn fled. Although she had no compunction about excavating all of his family secrets, he suspected she had a batch of her own.

REACHING THE KITCHEN, Brynn finally slowed down, her breathing labored. Jake McKenzie must think she's nuts.

Having him at the house was comforting in a way. But she hated to fall into the old trap of believing a man spelled safety. Concentrating on dinner, she collected the ingredients for enchiladas. After they were in the oven, Brynn prepared a simple flan that she hoped Andrea would like.

She set the table on the terrace. Sounds of chattering birds and leaves rustling in the breeze were preferable to the silence of the house. Andrea hadn't yet progressed to easy conversation—that would take a while. And Brynn wanted to alleviate the strain of forcing words not yet ready to be spoken.

Glancing out the wide kitchen window, she spotted Andrea and Jake approaching. The timer rang and Brynn pulled the enchiladas from the oven. The pungent aroma of cumin and cayenne scented the air, tempered by the tang of newly cut onions. Brynn enjoyed cooking. Another extension of her need to create, she supposed.

Her throat tightened as she thought of her daughter. From the time she could hold dishes and not drop them, Sarah had loved arranging the table. From simple lunches to elaborate teas, she had made their mealtimes special.

Hearing Jake and Andrea coming in the kitchen door, Brynn blinked away the sheen of tears. She saw a question forming in Jake's expression and forced her lips into a smile. "I've been chopping onions to sprinkle on the enchiladas. They're killer."

"What can we do?" Jake asked.

"Andrea, would you help yourself to iced tea?"

"Okay." She reached for the glass Brynn had

placed on the counter next to a dish of freshly cut lemon wedges.

It didn't take long to carry the simple supper and wine outside. As Brynn had expected, there wasn't much conversation during the meal. She knew she should fill the pockets of silence, but the memories were strong, pulling at her attention.

So she was startled when Andrea spoke. "Can I take Shamus for a walk?"

Although Andrea had managed only a few bites of her enchiladas, she'd eaten a little more than the day before. Catching Jake's gaze, Brynn nodded in agreement.

"Don't go far, Annie. The sun will be setting soon," Jake told his daughter. As she walked away, he turned back to Brynn. "Delicious dinner."

"Thank you."

Noticing that she was distracted, he picked up the bottle of wine, refilling her glass. He wondered if the mood was related to her earlier jumpiness. "You have a beautiful home."

"Thank you."

"I think Andrea's coming along," he commented.

Brynn smiled gently. "She's a lovely child."

Her words surprised him. "You can see that?"

"Yes. It's not all about today, not with troubled children… Not with any of us." Her fingers stroked the locket she wore.

His gaze followed the gesture. "Do you have a picture of your husband inside?"

Her fingers stilled. Reluctantly she opened the clasp to reveal two photos. "My late husband and daughter."

Appalled, he stared at her. "Both your husband and daughter are…?"

"Gone?" Her soft voice faltered for a moment, then steadied. "Yes."

Brynn didn't offer any details and he was loathe to probe into the painful subject. But he also hated having the tense silence continue. "Is that why you work with troubled children?"

"Yes. It's something I need to do."

And he thought he'd gotten a rotten deal when Val had left and Andrea's troubles started. Maybe his earlier speculation hadn't been so far off base. A loss that wrenching could have chased Brynn here. But maybe their deaths had been recent. Maybe this was the home they had shared. "Your daughter looks about the same age as Andrea."

Brynn swallowed again. ''She would be.''

Tragic as her situation was, Jake doubted Brynn would welcome pity. He wanted to ask how she had lived through such a horrible time, and how she survived each day. But he voiced neither question.

One of her cats wound between her ankles, eyeing him with suspicion. Virgil, as always, sat at Brynn's feet. It was as though she fortified herself with the pets. No wonder. Still, he doubted pets could completely fill the huge hole in her life.

He stretched out one hand for Virgil to sniff, wondering if the dog would growl at him. But Virgil simply watched his movement, accepting an awkward pat.

Brynn's small smile was tinged with sadness. ''He likes people.''

''He's always at your side. I thought he might not be partial to anyone else.''

''Animals are perceptive. They sense need. Virgil has stayed at my side since our first hours together. Much like Shamus is with Andrea.''

''She never had any pets,'' Jake admitted.

''Your ex-wife wasn't an animal lover?'' she guessed.

"Val thought they were annoying and messy."

Brynn stroked the dog's ears. "Pets never judge us. They don't hold grudges and they forgive most anything."

He wondered what Brynn felt she'd done that needed to be forgiven.

The second cat leaped up on Brynn's lap. He watched as she stroked the furry animal. Her hands were slender, graceful, articulate. Hands of an artist, he realized, picturing her at the potter's wheel, her long fingers stretching to mold the clay.

Did that fill the emptiness? he wondered. Could her art mean as much to her as family?

Catching her gaze, he glimpsed the pain in her eyes. Pain and vulnerability. It occurred to him that he'd unintentionally wandered past the point of uninvolved observer.

NEARLY A WEEK LATER Brynn cupped her hands over Andrea's as the child tried to master the potter's wheel. The cool, wet clay slipped between their fingers.

"Try not to think of catching the clay," Brynn urged. "It's not a runaway train. Make it a part of you and soon the wheel will have to catch up to you.''

Andrea's mouth was set in a determined line. ''It doesn't look this hard when you're doing it.''

''I've been potting for years.'' Brynn gradually lifted her hands away from Andrea's.

Although the clay wasn't forming into a definite shape yet, Andrea was starting to gain control. Brynn moved over to her own wheel. Working through the frustration of trying to form the clay was therapeutic. Both for Andrea and herself.

''Is this better?'' Andrea questioned.

''Much. You're developing a rhythm.''

Andrea kept her attention on the wheel. ''Really?''

Brynn smiled, the echo of another girl's voice in her mind. ''Really.''

''What are you making?''

Brynn looked at the clay forming beneath her hands. ''Today I'm making what you are.''

''A mess?''

Oh, that voice of yesterday. ''Just whatever evolves.''

''You mean it doesn't matter?''

"Exactly. Sometimes free expression is better than a carefully planned out piece."

"If you sell your stuff, how come you work with kids like me?"

Brynn swallowed the lump that wouldn't go away. "Because I need to."

"Oh. For the money?"

"No. For the emotional connection, to feel I'm giving back something."

"'Cause you don't have any kids?"

Her breath caught. Why did that question still hurt so sharply?

"Brynn, do you think the clay is going to turn out round when I'm done?" After a few moments of silence Andrea glanced up from the wheel. "Brynn?"

She pushed away the pain. "Do you want it to be round?"

"I sorta thought I'd try to make a bowl."

"That would be a good starting piece. It doesn't have to be perfect."

"You mean if it's got holes it wouldn't matter."

The young cut directly to the point. At least this one did. "Yes. Most beginners want to make something recognizable, but it's not easy."

"What did you make first?"

Brynn had never forgotten her first experience potting. She'd felt as if the wheel was an extension of her body, that she was meant to be one with it. "It wasn't so much what I made. It was how I felt that was worth remembering."

"Uh-huh." Andrea's tone was skeptical.

Brynn chuckled. "I'm not trying to scam you. My first attempt was a vase. It looked right, but it was a wobbler—it didn't sit evenly."

"You made the vases that are in the house, didn't you?"

"Most of them. Why?"

Andrea shrugged in reply.

Catching on, Brynn smiled. "We'll work on one to put in your house."

In the time she'd worked with the child, Andrea had progressed past Brynn's expectations. Reducing the meds had dispelled the dullness from her eyes and expression. And Shamus had pushed his way into Andrea's heart, his devotion open, easy to recognize.

However, Jake's reconnection to his daughter was still in the beginning stages. Taking a leave of absence from his job to stay with Andrea had been a huge step. But the relationship still needed work.

For the next while nothing could be heard but the whir of the wheels, the gurgle of water and the soft slap of hands on clay.

They were good, productive sounds, Brynn believed. The kind that comforted and sometimes healed. This was a time when she could imagine all was right with the world. And when that couldn't be achieved, she could believe that the healing of another person's child gave her back a bit of Sarah.

Footsteps, the masculine sound of leather heels on cool terrazzo tiles in the entry hall, joined the other noises. Jake's stride was so distinctive and certain. She'd noticed that from the first day—how it seemed as though he never faltered. Her husband had shared the same quality. Brynn had admired Kirk's strength of purpose and of character. Thoughts of the insinuations the police made dimmed the memory, and her smile faded. But Jake wasn't Kirk.

Her throat tightened. And Andrea wasn't Sarah. But Brynn's heart was finally expanding to include others.

As Jake's footsteps faded, she realized that scared her more than any threat.

CHAPTER SIX

HEARING THE CLIP-CLOP of hooves, Jake watched Roy leave the barn, leading one of the horses toward the corral. The stallion showed spirit, and Jake wondered who rode the animal. It clearly wasn't the mount for an amateur.

The older man tugged his hat in greeting.

"Morning, Roy. Nice looking animal."

"Yeah. One of the best of the lot. Graham Ford bought his granddaddy. Turned out to be a champion."

"Graham?"

"Julia's father." Roy closed his eyes and gave a little shake of his head.

"Brynn's friend." Jake was guessing, though he said it as though he knew this to be a fact.

Reluctantly, Roy nodded. "Aye."

"It wasn't easy bringing Andrea here. But Brynn's reputation is unmatched."

Roy simply grunted.

"She's already working miracles with Andrea."

Roy nodded slowly. "She's good with the kids."

There were a dozen questions Jake would have liked to ask the older man about Brynn, but he sensed they wouldn't be welcomed. Instead, he studied the horse. "You about to exercise him?"

"Yep. He's always first— I don't like being tuckered out when I take him on."

"Would you like a hand?"

Roy drew his eyebrows together again. "Won't take you away from your work?"

Jake found himself wanting to take the reins of this fine animal. "Nope."

Roy studied him for another moment, then handed Jake the thin strips of leather. "Suits me."

Jake felt the restrained power of the stallion as he held the reins. "What's his name?"

Already walking away, Roy glanced back over his shoulder. "Fortune."

Running one hand over the horse's muzzle, Jake lowered his voice. "So, boy, is that because you're worth a fortune or you cost one?"

Fortune swished his tail, ears alert, eyes watchful.

"Not sure who I am yet. That's okay. Just makes you smart as well as strong." Jake walked him to the corral. Opening the gate, he removed the bridle and watched the stallion take off.

Powerful legs pumped as Fortune danced around the corral. Head flung back, he seemed to be reaching for the sky. The beast was magnificent, Jake realized. An unexpected treasure in this sleepy part of the country.

Riding him would take skill. And Jake itched to learn if he still possessed enough. Rather than hitch Fortune to the exercise ring, Jake simply watched the stallion run.

He wasn't certain how much time had passed when he heard the soft thud of boots on the packed dirt.

"He's something to see," Roy commented quietly.

"Amazing." Together they observed the stallion for a few minutes before Jake turned to the older man. "Who rides Fortune?"

"No one much, anymore."

"Has Brynn put him out to stud?"

Roy kept his gaze on the horse. "Nope."

That seemed a huge waste, but it wasn't his concern. "I'd like to take him out sometime."

Glancing over, Roy appraised him. "Might be best not to go out alone the first time."

Jake had the discomforting sensation that Roy could see straight inside him to both his strengths and weaknesses. "Right."

"There's some desolate parts round here. A body could go undetected for weeks."

"A *body*?"

Roy shrugged. "Rider who gets thrown."

Despite the full sun overhead, Jake felt an unexpected chill. "Does Brynn ride alone?"

Roy nodded. "Doesn't make it smart."

No. But Jake suspected good sense wouldn't stop her.

The peaceful remoteness of the ranch could be too lulling, the surroundings discouraging caution. A second later he thought of all the times Brynn had bolted. Frowning, he wondered which image was more troubling.

A HORN HONKED, a cheery beep-beep, as a car approached. Despite the sudden fear gripping her, Brynn made sure her face was composed as she glanced at Andrea. "I'll see who it is." Leaving the studio, she headed to the front of the house. Jake was outside somewhere and his car was parked beneath the oak tree. The dogs were there as well, and she could hear them barking.

Heart racing, she pulled the curtain back a few inches.

Julia!

Relief flooded through her. It was so unlike her friend to drive up without phoning.

Brynn pulled open the door, a smile blossoming as she hurried down the steps. Julia was piling out of the car at the same time.

"Jules! What a surprise!"

Julia hugged her, then stepped back. "Your phone must be switched off or the battery's run down. And since I know you don't answer the ranch phone, I didn't even try that one."

Brynn covered the "oh" of surprise on her lips with one hand. "I haven't given the phone a thought in days."

Julia lifted her eyebrows. "Really?"

"I've been so caught up with Andrea, I suppose."

Looking a touch skeptical, Julia opened the rear door of her car, releasing Lobo to join the other dogs. "Only with Andrea?"

Brynn grimaced. Julia could be overprotective. "I'm beginning to wonder if it was such a good idea to tell you about Jake staying here."

When Julia glanced away briefly, Brynn felt a jolt of surprise. "Is that why you're here? To make sure that I haven't welcomed a serial killer into the house?"

"I can't help it. I've been *worried*. I know I'm the one who said he must be legit if he knew the Cranstons' doctor. But logic's harder to hang on to when I'm miles away."

Touched, Brynn smiled. "And when you're miles away we can't share Häagen-Dazs and a horseback ride."

"Not that we'd do those at the same time," Julia replied, her worry lines easing.

"Did you bring Shipley's doughnuts?" Brynn teased.

Julia shook her head. "I just jumped in the car and drove here."

Which meant her friend must have been terribly concerned. "I'm sorry to worry you. I honestly haven't given the phone a thought."

"It gave me a good excuse to visit."

"I'm awfully glad you did. I want you to meet Andrea. She's come so far this last week."

Julia's concerned look returned. "Brynn, you're not still comparing her to…"

An arrow of pain hit its mark. "Sarah? I don't think so."

Julia squeezed her arm. "I haven't been here ten minutes and I'm saying all the wrong things."

"It's good to have you here. Come on."

Together they entered the house. Although still reserved, Andrea was responsive to Julia. But then her friend's breezy manner usually appealed to kids.

Brynn placed a hand on Andrea's shoulder. "Why don't we take a break?"

Andrea agreed and Brynn suggested she look for her dad.

After the child left, Julia turned to Brynn. "She's very quiet, isn't she?"

"Yes. But she's so much better than when she arrived. I was frightened for her. Actually, I still am."

"Then she's in the right place," Julia replied loyally.

Brynn smiled. "Why don't we head outside? I think Roy's still here."

Julia's expression brightened. "Then my timing couldn't be better."

Having lost all of her own relatives, Julia treated her friends as extended family. And Roy had always been like a favorite uncle. He and Mary had no children of their own, and Julia was very special to them.

Finding Roy and Jake by the corral, where Andrea had joined them, Julia favored Roy with a warm hug before turning to Jake. "So, you're the man I haven't heard enough about yet."

Jake saw in a glance that Julia was both attractive and much less reserved than Brynn. "There's not that much to hear."

Her smile was speculative. "I doubt that."

Although her manner was flirtatious, he realized she wasn't interested in him. It was mainly habit, he suspected. But Jake also had the feeling that he was being checked out in a clearly nonsexual way.

Brynn looped her arm around Andrea's waist. "How do hamburgers cooked on the grill sound?"

"Okay."

Jake caught Brynn's gaze. "I'll get the fire going."

"There should be some mesquite just behind the main lean-to," Julia told him.

Finding the wood, he began building a fire in the massive brick barbecue pit. From his vantage point Jake watched Brynn. She kept Andrea beside her, including her in the adult conversation. Her hand remained on Andrea's shoulder. And as he watched, she ran her fingers over his daughter's ponytail, a tug of affection. The natural maternal gesture made his throat tighten. It was something his daughter had never experienced with her own mother. His ex-wife had always been concerned about sticky fingers and not mussing her designer clothes.

But then he hadn't expected his own leap of joy when he'd seen Andrea for the first time. Why hadn't he kept that joy alive for his child? Perhaps she wouldn't have suffered such a critical breakdown when Val left.

Jake thought of his own mother, always ready with a smile and hug. He had taken her devotion for granted. And when she'd passed away, he'd convinced himself that the ache he felt would be temporary. Instead, he'd filed that, too. Something he never examined. He shook his head. What was it about Brynn that had him delving into every painful memory he possessed?

The fire had a good start, the crisscrossed logs a sturdy foundation for the other kindling. It didn't take long for the smell of wood smoke to fill the air. The pit was positioned far enough away so as not to blast the terrace with either heat or smoke. Yet it was close enough that he could hear the sounds of the meal being prepared. Julia's tinkly laugh harmonized with Brynn's lower, huskier tones. And while Andrea didn't laugh, she was included in the conversation. That Julia chatted to her didn't surprise him. He wouldn't expect Brynn to choose a friend who'd be indifferent to a child.

He straightened up suddenly. Where had that thought come from? Why should he care about Brynn's choice of friends?

Aggravated with himself, he collected more firewood, wishing he had a sturdy tree trunk to split. He could use some mind-clearing physical labor.

After the hamburgers were cooked and everyone settled at the table, Jake was startled when Andrea spoke.

"Can you smell it, Dad?"

Shocked that she was initiating conversation, he stared for a moment before replying. "Smell what?"

"My perfume. Julia gave it to me." Her tone was one hundred percent teenager.

"Perfume? Aren't you—" As he started to protest, he caught Brynn's gaze. She nodded her head just enough to warn him not to disapprove. "Sophisticated," he amended.

Andrea smiled and his insides twisted. It was a smile he'd despaired he'd never see again.

"I just forget sometimes that you're growing up," he added.

Andrea didn't seem to mind this admission. But then, she had always been a gentle soul. It was the reason she'd been able to tolerate Val's indifference for so long.

Brynn and Julia both beamed at him. Being the lone male had its benefits, he supposed. He listened to the women chat over the meal, Andrea adding an occasional comment. Burgers eaten, Andrea left to feed the dogs and Julia disappeared inside to make a business call.

Alone with Brynn, Jake saw that she was studying him. "What?"

Her smile was knowing. "You needn't worry, you know."

"About what?"

"You're not about to be cuddled to death."

Whatever he'd guessed she'd say, it wasn't that. "Oh?"

"You had that purely male look of apprehension, as if you were afraid we'd go all gooey and hug you to pieces."

"I wasn't—"

"It's okay, Jake. Few men enjoy being outnumbered by women who are touched by a father's feelings for his daughter."

"That so?"

She smiled. "Not that I'm an expert. But Julia and I can restrain ourselves."

With a twinge he realized he wasn't particularly happy to hear that. "I didn't realize I was so transparent."

Her eyes grew serious. "You're not. This is a rare exception."

He wondered if she had been trying to see beyond the surface. "Communications 101?"

"Perhaps."

"The longer I'm here, the less I seem to know about you."

Brynn's throat worked and he could see the flutter of nerves in her neck. "Not everyone can be an open book."

But most aren't hermetically sealed.

Julia's footsteps sounded on the weathered tiles and Jake kept his thoughts to himself.

"Crisis averted," she announced, settling back into her chair. "So, Jake McKenzie. Tell me about yourself. I don't even know what you do for a living."

"By trade I'm an engineer."

"Hmm...sly, but I sense there's more."

"I head the international engineering division of Canyon Construction."

"Ah. So you travel a lot?"

Briefly he met Brynn's knowing gaze. "Afraid so."

"That must be difficult."

"It is now."

He expected Julia to pounce on that one, but she didn't. "But you enjoy your work?"

"Jake isn't the proverbial bug on your microscope slide," Brynn chided.

"Sorry," Julia replied, not looking very contrite. "But Brynn can tell you I'm impossibly curious."

Behind the breezy words, he suspected Julia was more than simply curious. "And what do you do for a living?"

If his turning the tables surprised Julia, she didn't show it. "PR. Anticipating the other half of that question—yes, I enjoy it. But every once in a while the pace gets to me."

"Oh, Julia, I didn't know that," Brynn interjected.

Her friend shrugged. "Just when I'm tired. Usually it's great. But sometimes at the end of the day, snuggling on the sofa sounds more appealing than facing another roomful of people.''

Brynn's face filled with concern, her empathy palpable. ''Why don't you stay here for a bit? Regroup and recharge.''

''That sounds incredibly tempting, but my calendar's jammed.''

Brynn put her hand over Julia's. ''You're not going to meet that special man to snuggle on the sofa with if you're too exhausted to notice him.''

As he watched, Julia's carefree facade faded. ''You're probably right. But I'm not ready to give up the big city just yet.''

''You know best. But at least stay until Sunday. That'll give you four days of complete R and R.''

''I'm tempted—''

Brynn leaned forward, her green eyes darkening. ''You're already here, Jules. Please? You know I'll worry endlessly otherwise.''

That seemed to do the trick, Jake observed.

''Fine. But I'll stay out of the way—''

''In your own home? I don't think so,'' Brynn asserted.

So this *was* Julia's ranch.

''But I don't want to interfere with Andrea's progress,'' Julia protested.

"You've already won her over. You'll be helping. Won't she, Jake?"

Caught unprepared by the question, he nodded. "Sure."

Julia's scrunched her features into a skeptical expression. "I'm not convinced of that, but I would like to see more of Roy and Mary. And the horses."

Brynn smiled in relief. "Good! That's settled."

Jake could see the close bond between the women. It struck him that Brynn seemed to inspire trust.

Something Val had never, ever done.

CHAPTER SEVEN

JULIA'S UNEXPECTED VISIT brought a dinner invitation from Roy and Mary Bainter. One that included Brynn, Jake and Andrea as well.

And Brynn was nervous. She hadn't socialized in months. But Julia's mood was high as they drove to the Bainters'. Despite her misgivings about dinner, Brynn was glad her friend had decided to stay for the weekend.

It didn't take long for the Land Rover to travel the short distance between the ranches. Julia kept up a stream of chatter the entire time. But Brynn found her own words evaporating.

Once at the Bainters', she fell completely silent as they stepped out of the vehicle. Glancing up, she saw that Jake was staring at her curiously. No doubt wondering what had gotten into her, she realized.

Luckily, the front door opened and Roy ambled out onto the porch. ''Mary's cooking up a storm.''

"I can't wait!" Julia replied, climbing the steps. Reaching the top, she hugged the older man.

Brynn trailed after her friend. Nerves increasing, she watched Julia greet Mary with another hug.

Then the older woman turned to Brynn. "You must be the lovely lady Roy's told me about."

Surprised by Mary's choice of words, Brynn felt the warmth of an unexpected blush. "How kind."

The older woman's eyes were wise, understanding. And Brynn realized that Julia's trust in the couple was well placed. "Not at all. I'm glad you could join us."

"Can I do anything to help?"

"Just relax. Roy is making drinks out on the back porch and everything in the kitchen's under control."

Although tense, Brynn smiled. "Thanks."

Mary turned her attention to Andrea and Jake, greeting them with equal warmth.

Brynn watched anxiously, but Andrea held up fine in the presence of yet another stranger. Mary took her under her wing, drawing Andrea into the kitchen and helping her feel at home.

Yet even after Brynn went out onto the back

porch, she continued to watch the girl through the open doors. Unable to settle her own anxiety, she felt it increase to include Andrea. It was still with Brynn as she sipped a drink, then wandered farther outside. Glancing back, she could glimpse Andrea in the kitchen.

"Take a breath," Jake told her quietly a few minutes later, joining her on the back lawn.

Brynn's gaze shifted. "It's so hard to know when they're ready to take the next step. I was afraid this might be too much for Andrea."

"She's starting to heal. Thanks to you."

Brynn's anxiety was still high. "Partially. Some of it's up to her. But the most important step is for you to take."

He looked puzzled. "And you don't think I'll do my part?"

Wanting so much for this girl, Brynn wavered between diplomacy and truth. "I know you'll do everything in your power right now because you've nearly lost her. But what about later on? Will the next project in Kenya mean more than Andrea's sense of stability?"

"That was a low blow."

"I didn't mean for it to be. I'm just trying to be realistic. Your job takes you far away. And I don't think Andrea can bear that anymore."

He blinked. "You're saying I have to choose between my career and my daughter?"

She bit her lower lip. She'd dreaded telling him this, but he had to face the truth at some point. "Not exactly. Surely you can find a way to do the same work without the extensive travel."

"If I want to give up a career I've worked for, sacrificed for!" Frustration hardened his expression.

"I wish there was an easier answer, but truthfully, I can't think of one. Andrea needs *you*— not a substitute. People can be hired to do most anything, but no one can raise and love your child the way you can."

Anger made his voice quiet, deliberate. "So what we're doing now is for nothing?"

She placed one hand on his arm. "Of course not. Your love is saving her, day by day, hour by hour. I don't mean to discount that in any way."

Jake glanced toward his daughter, still visible through the open double doors that led to the kitchen. "I plan to take off more time in the future, to make sure Andrea doesn't feel abandoned."

Brynn sighed. How could she make him understand that he couldn't schedule the nurturing Andrea needed? That love couldn't be computed and then dosed out at convenient times? But his tense expression told her he wasn't ready to hear that yet.

"You two look awfully serious for a barbecue," Julia commented. "I hope nothing other than the kabobs will be skewered."

Brynn shook off her somber feelings. "Of course not."

Julia glanced from her to Jake. "I could use a hand with the salad. You know I'm useless in the kitchen."

Actually, she wasn't, but Brynn took her hint. This wasn't the place for their weighty conversation. "I think I can tear up a few pieces of lettuce."

She wasn't certain, but Brynn suspected that Jake's gaze remained fixed on her back as she retreated. She also guessed the conversation had only been put on hold.

A FEW HOURS LATER, sated and sleepy, they were headed home. The night had an inky quality that made it seem as though they were alone on this stretch of land, safely tucked into the

Land Rover. It should be a cozy feeling, but Jake wasn't in a cozy mood.

Relieved when they reached the ranch, he immediately suggested that it was time for Andrea to turn in. After Brynn's bombshell, he wasn't keen on any more conversation.

Tired after an unusually long day, Andrea didn't protest the early night. Jake paced in his room, feeling trapped for the first time since he'd arrived. When he heard Brynn's door close, he opened his own and stalked down the stairs. But even the den wasn't large enough to lessen the feeling of confinement so he headed outside.

From the barn he could hear the neighing of horses as he walked to the empty corral. Leaning against the railing, he lifted his head. He needed something as big as the sky to steady his anger, he decided.

Footsteps sounded on the soft dirt and he sighed. He didn't need another confrontation with Brynn.

"That sigh sounded as big as our famous Texas sky," Julia commented.

Well, at least it wasn't Brynn. "I didn't know anyone else was out here."

She dusted her hands together. "Me neither. When I need to clear my head, I come out here.

And it's hard to find a better listener than one of the horses.''

"Yeah.''

Julia stepped closer. "At the risk of sounding nosy, I couldn't help overhearing part of your chat with Brynn tonight.''

He bit back a rude comment.

Julia apparently guessed that he had. "You're right. I shouldn't have eavesdropped, but I care about Brynn. I had to make sure she could hold her own.''

"If you overheard, then you know she did.''

"Which really pisses you off.''

"You're blunt.''

"Yeah. I get that a lot. Most people can't figure out how Brynn and I can be friends, since she's so gentle. But even though you're mad right now, I think you can understand. Sometimes it takes an opposite sort to keep us centered. Like you and Brynn. She's all warmth and caring and compassion. That's why she told you the truth tonight. She cares too much not to.''

"Is there any of my personal business you don't feel comfortable dragging out into the open?''

She shook her head. "Not really.''

He sighed again, but with less effort. "I care about my daughter."

"Obviously. Or you wouldn't be here. Now you've got to decide whether to stay mad at Brynn or accept her help."

He drew his eyebrows together. "In doing what? Ditching my career?"

"Not necessarily. See, that's the great thing about Brynn. She'll nudge you in the right direction, but ultimately the decision is yours."

"Suppose she told you it was best for you to completely give up your job, the life you'd carved out?"

Julia's expression softened. "She has."

Game point. "You haven't listened to her."

"Nope. But then, I don't have a beautiful daughter who adores me."

Game, set and match.

Julia rocked back on her well-worn boot heels. "And since Brynn once did, she doesn't want you to lose something so completely irreplaceable."

Jake swallowed, thinking of Brynn losing a daughter she loved as much as he did Andrea.

"Yeah." Julia's voice was quiet. "I'll say good night." She started to walk away, then turned back. "I wouldn't have said all this if Brynn didn't think you were such a good man."

And then she was gone. But her words seemed to echo in the vast darkness between earth and sky. Brynn thought he was a good man? Absurdly, Jake realized he valued those words more than any others he'd heard in years.

BRYNN FOUND HERSELF tiptoeing the next morning. Why had she brought up the subject of Jake's job? Probably the result of nerves, she realized. Had she blown all the trust she'd built up with him?

Jake's situation with Andrea was unique, in her experience. As a single father, his choices alone would determine the child's ultimate recovery.

With Virgil by her side, Brynn headed toward the barn. Julia was immersed in her sole obsession—her horses.

"Can I lure you inside for breakfast?"

Julia shook her head. "I had coffee and toast. How about a ride later?"

"If you're sure I won't hold you back."

Bending over, Julia inspected a hoof. "Nah. Do you want to ask Jake and Andrea to join us?"

She hesitated for only a moment. "Sure." Realizing it wasn't Julia she needed to speak with, Brynn returned to the house to prepare French toast, perhaps as much a comfort food for herself as to tempt Andrea.

When she heard footsteps in the hall connecting to the kitchen, she took a deep breath.

However, she didn't see any storm clouds on Jake's face when he passed through the open doorway.

"Smells good. French toast?"

Distracted, she glanced at the plate of warm, fragrant toast. "Yes, I—"

Andrea came in, going straight to the refrigerator. It had become a habit for her to pour the orange juice each morning.

Acting as though nothing was bothering him, Jake pulled a mug from the rack and poured some coffee. "Where's Julia?"

"Um, the barn. She wants us all to go for a ride later."

He tilted his head, apparently considering it. "Sounds okay. What do you think, Annie?"

"Sure. Brynn, can Shamus have a piece of bacon?"

"It's not good for him, sweetie. But you can give him a piece of carrot."

"I still can't believe the dogs like carrots," Andrea commented, pulling one out and snapping off a piece.

"It's what they're used to," Jake commented. "They think it's a treat."

"Yes, right," Brynn mumbled.

Breakfast seemed agonizingly long as Brynn considered what to say to Jake.

"Aren't you hungry?" he asked, looking at her full plate.

Brynn glanced down at her forgotten food. "Not really."

"Can I help Julia with the horses?" Andrea asked.

"Sure, yes. That would be fine," Brynn replied, still distracted.

Once Andrea had headed to the stable, Brynn balled her napkin into a wad and bit her lip. "Um, Jake..."

"Yes?"

"I want to apologize for bringing up...for bringing up the subject of your career at an inappropriate time."

"Okay."

Okay? She'd spent the night tossing and turning, realizing the mistake she'd made, its possible repercussions.

"But—"

"Don't worry about it." Jake shoved back his chair, the legs scraping against the floor. "Do you want a hand with the dishes?"

"I, um, I can do them."

"I'll be outside then."

Staring after him, she wondered what had just happened. Had his anger somehow dissipated in the night?

The thought plagued her as she stacked the dishes in the dishwasher, and later, as she changed into her riding gear. But when she walked outside, she was overcome by the happy picture that Jake, Julia and Andrea made. Her friend was bringing out the best in Andrea. And Jake, as well. Ignoring a ridiculous spurt of jealousy, Brynn smiled brightly. "Looks like you're all set."

"Now that you're here," Julia replied, her eyes warm.

And Brynn was immediately ashamed of her petty feelings.

"Is Honey okay with you?" Julia continued.

Julia had chosen a horse that was both biddable and intelligent. "Perfect." Brynn noticed then that both Fortune and the gelding, Destiny, were saddled. Usually no one but Julia rode the two more spirited animals. Gentle Lizzie was also saddled, presumably for Andrea.

Jake unhooked Fortune's reins from the hitching rail.

"He has a lot of spirit," Brynn blurted, concerned that Jake couldn't control the horse.

Both Julia and Jake looked at her in surprise.

Julia spoke first. "I warned him, but he's game."

The sense of fear she'd never escaped since Sarah's death brushed her now. "Oh."

Jake met her gaze. "I respect him. And I'm not a novice."

She breathed a little easier. "Good."

As they began the ride, Brynn saw that Jake hadn't exaggerated. He sat the horse as though he rode daily. Foolish for her to worry, she realized. Strange, too. And unlike her. She hadn't fretted about anyone other than close friends, family and the children she mentored since Sarah's death.

While Jake and Julia forged the trail, Brynn kept a close eye on Andrea, but the girl was enthusiastic about the ride, the horses and even the land they crossed.

The day was perfect for riding. The sky was clear and the sun wasn't yet too intense. Beef cattle grazed on the open range. A few lifted their heads in mild curiosity as the riders passed.

The land grew rugged, the trees sparser as they climbed the brow of a hill. But the terrain didn't faze Jake or Julia. Brynn glanced at Andrea. As she recovered, the child's spirit reminded her even more of Sarah. To lose her again… She couldn't finish the thought.

But Andrea didn't push her horse, content to stay beside Brynn. "How come Julia has so many horses if she doesn't live here?"

"Because she loves them. And she knows that Roy takes good care of them."

"Kind of like your dogs? You can't play with all of them at the same time, but you still like them?"

Brynn smiled at the comparison. "Good example. I couldn't imagine my life without them."

Andrea's expression grew a little sad. "I don't have a dog at home. My mom never wanted one."

Brynn ached for this child who had asked for so little and had apparently received even less from her mother. "Not everyone can relate to animals."

"Yeah. I guess." But Andrea's expression was still glum.

"You, on the other hand, have a natural gift. Shamus took to you from the first moment he saw you. And all the other animals like you, too."

Andrea smiled shyly. "I really like Shamus."

Even though she would miss him, Brynn decided she would give Andrea the dog if Jake allowed it. Both Andrea and Shamus would be happier together. But it was something she would have to ask Jake another day.

They pushed on, covering more ground. However, Brynn began to grow concerned. Andrea looked pale. Reining in her horse, Brynn reached over, placing her other hand over Andrea's, slowing Lizzie. "How are you feeling, Annie?"

Andrea hesitated.

"It's all right, sweetie. We're going to stop." Keeping her tone calm, Brynn called for the others, who turned back.

"We need to rest," she told them when they were close enough to hear.

Understanding immediately, they dismounted. Julia took the reins and Jake walked to his daughter's side, steadying her as she shakily slid to her feet.

Brynn took the bedroll from behind her saddle and spread it on the ground. Then she retrieved her canteen.

"I didn't realize we were overdoing it," Jake told her, his eyes filled with worry and guilt.

"I didn't, either," Brynn reassured him. "Not until just now."

He pushed back his hat, studying Andrea's too-white face.

"Would a snack help?" Julia asked. "I packed sandwiches and apples."

"The sugar in the apple would probably help the most," Brynn replied.

Julia hurried off to get the food, and Jake dug in his pocket, producing a knife. "I'll cut it up in pieces the way you liked when you were little, Pooh."

Andrea's eyes remained closed. "Okay, Daddy."

Brynn watched the emotions play over his face. No matter what choices he may have made in the past, Jake McKenzie loved his daughter.

At his urging, Andrea ate a few bites of apple. It took a while, but he talked her into eating part of a sandwich, as well. Some color returned to her cheeks and Brynn felt a trace of relief. Although Andrea had come extremely far in the past weeks, she had been dangerously fragile. And even after easing off the heavy medications she'd been on, she was still delicate, vulnerable.

Impulsively, Brynn placed her hand over Jake's, offering her support. His eyes, unguarded, met hers, and she glimpsed the secrets that made up Jake McKenzie. Secrets that held pain, and yes, regret.

Sharing something that deep, that personal, shook her. That kind of connection was one she'd shared only once before.

Jake turned his hand so that he now held hers. Despite her own panic, she couldn't ignore the entreaty in his eyes. And her fingers remained fast within his.

IT TOOK A FEW HOURS longer to retrace their path to the ranch. Jake took great care to make certain he didn't lead too quickly. His anxiety was painful to watch, yet Brynn's gaze was drawn to him again and again.

Luckily, Andrea held up well on the return trip. They took more breaks than she probably needed, and they were all relieved when the house was finally in sight.

Julia offered to stable the horses so that Jake and Brynn could take care of Andrea. Some of the child's inherent resiliency had returned. Still, after a warm bath, she was ready for bed.

Jake hovered, hesitating to leave Andrea alone. Brynn finally clasped his arm, gently urging him out of the room. She left the door open so they could hear if she cried out.

"She'll be all right," Brynn whispered, once they were out in the hall.

Jake walked slowly downstairs with her. Brynn poured two glasses of wine, offering him one. He emptied his quickly. Brynn didn't comment as she refilled the glass he held out.

With his other hand, Jake rubbed his forehead. "I can't believe I know so little about my own daughter."

"I don't understand."

"I should have seen that she couldn't take that much exertion."

"Actually, I was the one who should have known," Brynn argued. "I'm the one who has worked with troubled kids." She paused. "But before we heap too many ashes on our heads, I think she'll be fine. She may be tired for a few days—"

"I want to take her to the city tomorrow, have the doctor check her out."

Brynn thought it was overkill, but she nodded. "Whatever you think is best."

"I think we've established that I don't know what's best. But I'll feel better if she sees the doctor."

Brynn thought of her ill-advised words the previous day at the Bainters. Even though she knew Jake would have to come up with a solution for balancing his family and career, her comment had been premature. "You're her father. And in the end, that's what matters most."

"You're a hell of a woman, you know that?" He stepped a bit closer.

At the moment Brynn was having a difficult time knowing anything. "I should help Julia with the horses...."

He held her gaze for so long she thought she'd forget to breathe. Then that rare, total honesty in his eyes disappeared. "You stay here with Andrea. I'll rub down the horses."

"No. If she wakes, she'll want you." Not waiting for an answer, she fled.

Into the night. Into the darkness that masked her regret. Why had she run from such openness, a gift that he probably wouldn't share again?

It was so still as she left the house that she

could hear Julia talking to the horses in the barn, her clear voice floating on the faint breeze.

Emotionally and physically weary, Brynn stumbled, then caught herself. Julia was equally tired, yet she wouldn't complain. Shaking herself, Brynn took a deep breath, then entered the barn.

Julia looked up. "How's Andrea?"

"Tired, but okay, I think."

"Geez, I feel terrible. I never should have suggested that ride."

"Another candidate willing to take on my responsibility," Brynn muttered. "Julia, *I* should have realized Andrea's limits. Not you, not Jake."

Julia looked at her mildly. "Who put a wasp in your underwear?"

Against all reason, Brynn laughed.

Even Lizzie turned her head to watch.

Weakly, Brynn clutched her side. "I wasn't expecting that."

"Even you can't anticipate everything. Sounds like Andrea's going to be okay."

"Jake's going to take her to the doctor tomorrow."

"Old Doc Riley in Walburg?" Julia questioned, referring to the sole practitioner in town.

Brynn shook her head. "Nope. They're going to San Antonio."

"Oh, I see. Don't take it personally, Brynn. Fathers tend to freak over their daughters. I seem to remember that Kirk took Sarah to the emergency room when she was a baby because he thought some of her toes were too close together."

Brynn chuckled softly at the memory. "And he didn't really believe the doctor when he said they were normal."

Julia patted Lizzie. "These horses are about as close as I'll probably get to parenthood, but I know you're the best, Brynn. You give everything you have to give. Andrea's lucky that you took her on."

"You're prejudiced," Brynn protested weakly.

"Darn right I am. That's the point of friendship, isn't it? To have someone who's always on your side?" Julia hesitated. "Speaking of which, you going to be okay on your own tomorrow while they're gone?"

Brynn nodded. "I have a million things to catch up on. And it's not like the house will be empty, with all my pets here."

Julia's expression was understanding. "Okay then."

Brynn picked up a brush, happy to concentrate on the simple physical labor of caring for the horses. Perhaps it would keep her from thinking too hard about the man inside her home. At least for now.

JAKE AND ANDREA LEFT early in the morning. Julia wasn't far behind. Waving goodbye, Brynn considered her solitude. She was behind on the pieces consigned for her primary gallery. And she hadn't yet found time to go through all the mail Julia had brought on her previous visit.

Yet she was restless as she wandered through the house. Despite her assurances to Julia, it felt empty. Virgil shadowed her as usual. Bert and Ernie played tag up and down the stairs, causing the other dogs to make plenty of noise. Yet there was a loneliness to the place that hadn't been there before she'd taken on Andrea. Or her father.

"Get a grip," Brynn muttered, remembering when the other children had departed. There was usually a sense of satisfaction coupled with some relief. It had meant time she could use to reclaim the solitude she needed to regroup. She had none of those feelings now.

Of course, Andrea would return, Brynn told herself. That must be it—a sense of a mission not yet completed. Virgil nudged her hand and she bent down to pat his silky head. "Well, boy, it's just us for the rest of the day." Hearing the cats yowl upstairs, she winced. "And your unruly siblings, of course."

Eventually Brynn settled in her studio, but the hours passed fitfully. Her attention wandered from her work. She alternated from firm belief that Andrea was perfectly fine to thinking that the girl had been admitted to the hospital and Jake simply hadn't called to tell her the devastating news.

She fed the animals, but was too worried to eat anything herself. When she spotted Roy in the corral, she escaped outside, hanging around on the pretense of helping him until he left. Yet more hours remained in the day. More than she could fritter away.

It was after sunset when she heard a vehicle approaching. Disregarding caution, she flung open the door and rushed outside, the dogs close behind.

Andrea jumped from the car, smiling when

Shamus leaped up to greet her. "Hey, you miss me?" He barked and she gave him a hug.

Jake closed his car door. He looked relaxed, too, but Brynn had to know. "What did the doctor say?"

"That she overdid it a bit, but with no lasting effects."

Brynn released a sigh of relief.

"We'd have been back earlier, but we didn't want to come home empty-handed," he explained.

Puzzled, Brynn watched as he reached into the back seat, surfacing with several pizza boxes. "Oh my."

"We couldn't decide which one you'd like," Andrea told her. "So we got a bunch of different kinds."

Brynn saw the enthusiasm and expectation in her face. Touched by the child's gesture, she felt the sting of tears. *Silly,* she told herself. "I'll wager you brought at least one of my favorites."

"The man in the shop said they reheat well in the oven," Jake said as he shut the car door.

"I haven't had pizza in ages," Brynn admitted.

"So it's a good surprise?" Andrea asked.

"It's a *perfect* surprise! Thank you, Annie."

"You should have people do nice things for you," the child replied. "'Cause you're always doing neat stuff for everybody."

Brynn's throat worked and she hugged Andrea. As she did, Shamus barked, running in a circle. And that made Andrea laugh. It was a wonderful sound.

Above Andrea's head, Brynn met Jake's gaze. In the gathering dusk, she thought she glimpsed an opening there. Perhaps he hadn't shut the door, after all.

CHAPTER EIGHT

IN THE FOLLOWING DAYS, Jake watched Brynn work with Andrea. Clearly the riding incident had alarmed Brynn. Her natural compassion deepened; her words and gestures were even more maternal. And Andrea continued to bloom under her care.

But an unwelcome thought intruded into this bliss. How would his daughter cope once they left the ranch? And could he hope to step into the vacancy left by Brynn and rebuild his relationship with Andrea?

Brynn's smile as she glanced across the SUV was warm, inclusive. Now that Andrea was feeling better, Brynn had suggested a picnic lunch. But rather than walk to the spot she had in mind, they agreed it would be safer to drive so that Andrea wouldn't get too tired.

''It's just past the curve.'' Brynn pointed to a small copse of trees. It was an ideal location—

elevated just enough to provide a view of the surrounding countryside.

After parking, Jake opened the rear of the vehicle. The dogs jumped out, happy to be freed. As he reached for the hamper and small cooler, Brynn picked up an old quilt she had brought along.

Andrea collected the water jug and bowls for the dogs, her attention focused on Shamus, as usual. "He likes picnics, too, huh, Brynn?"

"You're right. All the dogs like an unfamiliar bit of land to investigate."

"Don't you take them to new places?" Andrea asked.

Brynn hesitated and Jake saw a cloud cross her face. "Not that much. I...keep very busy at the studio."

Andrea shrugged as they crossed to the level spot beneath the trees. "I'd go someplace different every day."

They were encouraging words, but Brynn smiled hesitantly and said nothing.

She and Andrea spread the quilt on the ground. Wild grass made a soft pad and Jake watched as Brynn showed Andrea how to check for rocks that might pierce the cloth.

"Do you picnic here often?" he questioned.

She shook her head. ''Not really. It's Julia's favorite place for a quick retreat. I haven't spent a lot of time researching picnic areas—'' her glance shifted to include Andrea ''—but I thought we could use a break in the routine.''

If he'd chosen to live in such an isolated area, Jake knew he'd want to explore every inch. Brynn didn't seem to lack curiosity. So why hadn't she ventured out much beyond the perimeters of the house?

As he continued to study her, Brynn unpacked the hamper, including Andrea in the task, creating an opportunity for her to interact.

He sniffed appreciatively. ''I've been drooling over that fried chicken since we left the house.''

Brynn smiled proudly. ''Your daughter's handiwork.''

''Well, not by myself,'' Andrea protested.

''I provided a little guidance. You were the chef,'' Brynn insisted.

''I used to cook some,'' Andrea admitted.

Before Val had deserted them, Jake thought Andrea had often prepared special dishes, delighting in surprising him. He swallowed, hating to think of how everything had deteriorated since then. ''Andrea makes the best Rice Kris-

pies treats in the world. She has a secret ingre-
dient.''

''Peanut butter,'' she admitted, surprising
him. ''And sometimes I put chocolate frosting
on top.''

Brynn and Andrea exchanged a smile. Then
Brynn turned back to the hamper to retrieve the
potato salad. As Andrea distributed the plates
and forks, Jake unpacked the soft drinks.

He didn't have to fake his praise of the food.
And he was gratified to see that Andrea ate a bit
more than usual.

''I'm stuffed,'' he admitted at last, after man-
aging second helpings.

''Not too full for dessert?'' Andrea asked.

Since her eyes were filled with an eagerness
that the thought of dessert alone couldn't cause,
he shook his head.

Twisting around, she reached into the bottom
of the hamper, coming up with a plastic con-
tainer. She peeled the lid back and put it aside.
Then she held out the rectangular dish, a look
of anticipation on her face.

''Your special Rice Krispies treats?''

Her smile grew. ''Uh-huh.''

He took one and bit into the chewy, gooey
bar. ''It's even better than I remembered.''

Andrea's smile spread across her face. And his heart tightened. Impulsively, he leaned forward, pulling her close.

She didn't shrink away, instead hugging him back. "I'm glad you like them, Daddy."

He cleared his throat as he released her. Glancing up, he saw tears in Brynn's eyes.

The dogs, off by the creek below, began barking. Brynn turned toward the sound. "They're probably chasing a rabbit."

Andrea scampered to her feet. "I'd better check on them."

Jake watched as she loped down the hill, looking so much stronger than before. "I can't believe the change in her."

"It's wonderful to watch," Brynn replied softly.

"Why the tears?"

"I suppose it's a womanly thing. It's hard to witness pure love such as yours and Andrea's without crying a little."

"I don't want to open any wounds, but are you reminded of your daughter at times like these?"

Her lips trembled a fraction as she nodded. "She loved her father so much. It was so difficult for her when she lost him."

Shocked, he stared at her. "They didn't die together?" He'd just assumed it was one horrible accident.

New tears glistened. "No. Kirk was killed in a car accident. Sarah's…death…was about three months later." Pain, still fresh, suffused her face.

"I'm sorry, Brynn. I shouldn't have asked."

"No. It's all right." She wiped her eyes. "Actually, I need to talk about Sarah. I hate to act as though she never existed. When people talk about moving on after a loss, I want to scream that I never intend to forget my child. And closure…what's that supposed to be? It's a tidy expression, but it means nothing. I was her mother, I was supposed to protect her from everything. It was my job, my duty, my *right!*" Breathing raggedly, she sucked in more air. "No one tells you that there'll be a hole in your heart forever."

Jake pulled her awkwardly into his arms, unable to let her suffer alone. She laid her head against his shoulder and he felt the hot dampness of more tears.

He registered that the dogs' barking seemed to come from a long way away, mingled with the cry of a hawk, and that the lazy afternoon breeze blew gently. His touch clumsy, he stroked

Brynn's long, loose hair, the thick waves soft beneath his hands.

The tears eased a little at a time. There was no great shudder of release, but rather a gradual stilling of her trembling body. She was warm, he realized. And soft. A very feminine woman.

The thoughts weren't appropriate, yet he wasn't surprised by them. It was difficult to ignore the glint of Brynn's eyes, the curve of her chin as it rested against his shoulder. He could see the fringe of her lashes, the faint freckles on the bridge of her nose.

She pulled back, her eyes dark with pain. "I'm not sure what came over me."

"I'd need to talk about Annie, too, if…"

"I know." She sat up a bit straighter, looking faintly embarrassed, yet determined. "But we're not going to lose her."

No. Brynn would fight to save her. He knew that for a certainty. "Do you want to tell me about Sarah?"

Brynn hesitated. "She was so beautiful—her spirit, I mean. She was gentle and kind and thoughtful. I don't know if it was because she was an only child, but she was always ready to spend time with me. Not like some kids, who can't be bothered. And when Kirk died, I thought I would, too. But Sarah shouldered half the responsibility as though she were an adult. I was so proud of her. It seemed that together we could face anything.'' The glow on her face began to fade and for a short while only birdsong and the rustle of leaves filled the air. "I miss her so much.''

"You've taken her loss and given it meaning. I don't know how many other kids you've saved, but I'm guessing Sarah's pretty proud of you.''

Brynn's eyes shone suddenly and she pressed her lips together. "I would give the world to see her smile one more time, to hug her again.'' This time the tears were silent, a few small drops that slipped over her cheeks.

Reaching out, he eased his thumb across her skin, wiping away the tears, wishing he could do the same for her pain. "I don't know the right things to say....''

She smiled, a touchingly painful smile. "Saying something, anything, is better than silence. Most people think they can't find the right words, so they avoid saying anything at all. And that's the worst.''

Her strength and beauty remained, despite the overwhelming pain. He met her eyes and wondered how this woman had come to possess so little pretense. Her face was close, so very close. Without plan, without expectation, he lowered his mouth to hers. Her lips, soft and sweet, registered surprise.

This time, when his fingers slid into her hair, his grasp was more urgent. Yet he didn't deepen the kiss to push into new territory, not yet defined.

Her eyes filled with questions as he released her mouth. "Don't make me apologize for that, Brynn. I'm not sorry."

She placed two fingers against her lips, then removed them slowly. "No. But I'm confused."

And she wasn't alone.

A sudden chorus of barking dogs intruded on the moment. Brynn turned, collecting plates and dumping their remains into the trash bag. He recognized the defensive gesture. But then, he didn't want to explain a kiss to Andrea, either.

"Whew!" Andrea exclaimed, plopping down on the quilt.

Jake narrowed his gaze. "Where have you been to get so tired out?"

"I followed the dogs," she explained. Glancing up, she met twin gazes of concern. "Not very far. Just down the stream a little way. They saw something—a rabbit, I think, like Brynn said.''

Jake frowned. ''It's not a good idea for you to go off on your own.''

''I wasn't by myself. I was with the dogs,'' Andrea stated logically.

He decided not to press the issue. It had been a good day for her and he didn't want to spoil it. ''You two about ready to head back?''

Brynn nodded, still busy repacking the hamper.

''Okay,'' Andrea agreed.

Back in the SUV, he drove toward the house. Sparing a glance at Brynn, he found her gaze meeting his. And it unsettled him all over again.

THE FOLLOWING DAY, Jake ambled from the post office to the hardware store. Walburg was small enough that it seemed easier to walk from place to place rather than repark the truck. Unlike some small towns that fell into disrepair, Walburg was a clean, tidy village. People were friendly. As a stranger he was noticed, but he saw only looks of curiosity.

A bell tinkled as he opened the door of the hardware store. Inside, he spotted the expected rows of tools and accessories. Larger items hung on the walls and the aisles were crowded with bins and barrels of gadgets.

The clerk, or possibly the proprietor, he realized, was helping the one other customer. Jake located the light switch he'd come for. As he waited at the counter, he noticed a poster: Grange Dance and Raffle. Saturday. 8:00 p.m. Old Livery.

He mulled the idea over. Brynn in a dress... It was surprising how the picture appealed to him.

The clerk, finished with the previous customer, turned to him. "You find everything you need?"

Jake nodded, his eyes still on the poster. Then he glanced up. "Yes, thanks."

"You thinking about going to the dance?"

Jake blinked. This *was* a small town. "I'm not sure."

"Everybody's invited. There's a raffle to raise money for the school."

"I see."

The clerk squinted at the cash register. "That'll be five dollars, twelve cents. If you want raffle tickets, they're two dollars each."

Jake reached into his pocket for the money. "I'll take three."

The man smiled and pulled the tickets off a roll on the counter. "Write your name on the tickets and put them in the barrel."

Jake filled in his name, Andrea's and Brynn's.

"You new to the area or just passing through?" The clerk popped open a paper bag and dropped the switch inside. "I know everybody round these parts. Haven't seen you before."

"I'm staying for a while," Jake replied.

"Then think about the dance. The kids always love it."

"Kids?"

"Sure. It's a family affair. Newborns to great-grannies."

Beyond school functions, the dances in Jake's experience involved low lights, good music, sophisticated women. Then again, this was Walburg. "Thanks. I'll think about it."

The man extended his hand. "Steve Peterson." *As in Peterson Hardware.*

"Jake McKenzie. Good to meet you."

Another customer opened the door, and Jake left. It didn't take long to drive back to the ranch or to replace the broken switch in the upstairs hall. But Peterson's words were taking root.

A walk after dinner had become a habit for

the three of them. And Jake waited until then to air the suggestion.

Andrea's reaction was skeptical. "A dance that *everybody* goes to? Even old people?"

Jake chuckled. "Even people as old as Brynn and me."

Andrea swished a long stick through the grass. The blades sprung back up, with a gentle swaying movement. "Parents aren't supposed to go to dances."

Brynn smiled. "When I was in junior high I probably would have been horrified by that, too. It was bad enough that the teachers went to the dances."

"Yeah." Andrea's response was heartfelt.

Jake held up his hands. "Don't gang up on me, ladies. Just think about it this week. By Saturday night it might sound more appealing than counting your freckles."

"Oh, Dad!"

Brynn didn't reply at all. But then he had a week to persuade her.

BY FRIDAY BRYNN WAS nearly at the end of her rope. She had said no in every gracious way she could think of. However, she did want Jake and Andrea to go. She had convinced Andrea it might be fun to meet other kids, believing this first step back into socializing would be good for the child. But Brynn hadn't expected Andrea to take the same words and use them on her.

And Jake was relentless. According to him, she needed to get out, meet some of the people in town. The thought both frightened and intrigued Brynn. What if her cover was blown?

But it would be interesting to meet the people of Walburg. Julia often spoke of the hardy German and Polish immigrants who had settled the area. Much of the land was still owned by the descendents of those same families. People of the earth—determined, committed folks. Ones she would probably enjoy knowing.

And it had been so long since she'd been anywhere…. But she kept remembering the reason for her seclusion. Still…with her confidence boosted by Jake's presence, their walks had grown longer. They ventured by car to virtually every bit of Julia's property. And Brynn couldn't help longing for a normal evening. To put on a dress…to feel like a woman again.

Briefly she touched her lips, remembering Jake's kiss. It had been a complete surprise, a shock, even. But she'd been reminded of feelings she thought had died with Kirk.

Her future had been a dark hole for so long she couldn't picture anything else. Staying alive had been her main focus after Sarah's death. But the pain on her own mother's face had convinced Brynn she had to try. She couldn't inflict the same horror on her.

But other than helping troubled children, Brynn hadn't found a purpose in life. Inspiration for her art was still mercurial, fleeting at best. But now she'd met Jake and Andrea....

Oh, she had become attached to this child. Julia's warning echoed in her thoughts. Yet Brynn couldn't help the feeling. Despite emotional similarities to Sarah, Andrea was her own person, one Brynn grew closer to each day. Andrea would claim a special place in her heart long after the girl left the ranch.

Leaning forward, Brynn opened her jewelry box. She took out a locket, the one her mother had given to her to wear at her first school dance. She remembered Billy Grant's father driving them to school and the love in her mother's eyes as she'd watched them go.

Andrea needed that same maternal concern. If they went to the dance, Brynn could step into the role this one time, be there for Andrea.

It was more of a recognition than a decision.

And the fear didn't seem to matter as much. With the locket nestled in her fingers, Brynn gently dislodged Bert from her lap. It was time to tell Jake and to find just the right thing for Andrea to wear.

BY SATURDAY EVENING the atmosphere was close to giddy. Brynn and Andrea had examined every piece of clothing in every closet in the house. Luckily, Julia kept a good assortment of clothes at the ranch. Pairing a cute top from Julia's collection with a skirt Andrea had packed, the girl looked perfect, Brynn decided.

"Do I look okay?" Andrea asked again after they arrived at the livery.

"Very much so," Brynn replied, her throat catching at the sudden anxiety overtaking Andrea. She lightly touched the locket that now rested on Andrea's neck. "If you get nervous, just rub the locket and remember what I told you." Gently she tugged Andrea's ponytail. "Okay?"

"Okay."

Jake put one hand on Andrea's shoulder. "You're a knockout, Annie."

"You're just saying that." But she looked pleased.

Pickup trucks and SUVs filled the usually quiet Main Street. And Walburg was decked out for the festivities, with miniature white lights strung on the trees lining the sidewalk. The large double doors of the livery were flung open. Old-fashioned lanterns hung on the walls, and bales of hay were stacked for seating. A group of local musicians played country and western tunes that could be heard above the buzz of conversation.

As they entered, Andrea clung closely to Jake and Brynn. But she relaxed a bit when she saw the informal gathering. Some families stood together. Others had split up, the women talking with one another, the kids running off to find other children their age. Many of the teenagers radiated toward the same spot on one side of the livery.

Brynn leaned close to Jake, her voice quiet. "Maybe if we walk over to the other kids her age…"

Jake nodded and led the way.

Once near the group, Brynn squeezed Andrea's hand in encouragement. "You can mingle if you'd like. And we'll be right here." Glancing up, she saw Mary Bainter headed their way.

After a big smile and warm hugs, the older

woman shuttled Andrea over to the group of kids, making introductions.

Brynn and Jake watched anxiously, but after a few nervous moments, Andrea began to blend with the others.

"I never thought I'd break into a sweat over a barn dance," Jake admitted.

"It's not the dance, it's Andrea," Brynn reminded him gently. "We're both worried."

So they were. "Thirsty?"

"Positively parched," Brynn replied.

He collected two cups of punch and wove back through the crowd with them. As he approached Brynn, she stood in profile. He remembered wondering how she'd look in a dress. He also remembered how he'd felt when she had emerged earlier that evening.

She'd chosen a dress that bared her back, its skinny straps resting on tanned shoulders. He didn't know much about women's clothing, but he doubted the deceptively simple dress could be purchased outside of Dallas or Houston. With her thick blond hair swept up into a ponytail, Brynn could have passed for a teenager herself.

Funny. He sensed she was as nervous as Andrea. Brynn turned as he approached, and he was struck again by her grace, her unusual beauty.

She certainly didn't resemble an earth muffin to-night. So who was she? Mentor and protector of children, grief-stricken widow, lady of mystery? As much as he wanted to unlock her secrets, Jake felt an equal need to protect her. He didn't know what from, but he sensed a vulnerability of immense proportions. Not that she was weak. Far from it. But beneath the strength, he suspected she cared almost too much. It could be a debilitating attribute.

Closer now, he saw a flicker of relief in her eyes when they connected with his.

She accepted the paper cup. "Thanks."

"You can repay me with a dance."

An "oh" of surprise mingled with uncertainty in her expression.

"I hadn't planned on dancing," she said after a moment, her lips moist from the punch she'd just sipped.

"Not even at a dance?" he teased mildly, wishing he could wipe the uncertainty away.

"Said that way, I suppose I sound ridiculous."

"Nah. Confused, maybe…"

She smiled, a small concession.

He took her cup and put it along with his in a trash barrel. Then he held out his hand.

Brynn hesitated, and he was nearly certain her fingers trembled as he closed his around them.

A country song about love lost wasn't unusual; it was expected, in fact. But Jake didn't expect the sharp tug of awareness when Brynn fitted into his arms. Sure, it had been a while since his divorce. But the newness of the feelings, like the anticipation of a first kiss, caught him off guard.

His steps were measured, moving to the slow tempo of the song. Her head was beneath his chin. He breathed deeply. She wasn't a perfume girl. Instead, the smell of warm sunshine permeated her hair, along with a slight hint of wild roses.

Sophistication and simplicity.

In Brynn the two didn't battle each other.

She tilted her head back a fraction, her green eyes flecked with pinpoints of light. More than the softness of her body, the lure of silky skin, her eyes pulled at him.

He didn't need this. Not in any way, shape or form.

Another couple bumped into him, pushing him even nearer to Brynn. This close to her he saw her throat work, watched as her lips parted.

But the barn dance that had created this moment also prevented its exploration. His daughter stood at the side of the room, as did new acquaintances, Brynn's neighbors.

Regret was heavy, heavier than expected.

Brynn's gaze lingered on his. Questions filled her eyes. But as he watched, a door closed and she turned, searching until she spotted Andrea.

"She's doing okay," he murmured.

"I just wanted to be sure."

"Is that all?"

She swallowed again, but didn't speak.

The song ended and, reluctantly, he released her hand.

Steve Peterson, the man Jake recognized from the hardware store, stepped up on the makeshift stage, carrying a barrel. "I could keep everybody on the edge of their seats, but I think we'd better get on with the raffle." He leaned forward, a mock-stern expression on his face. "Unless I can put the squeeze on anyone, talk 'em into buying more raffle tickets."

This elicited a groan from the crowd, scattered with assorted chuckles.

"That's what I thought." He turned to the woman beside him, who looked like a cross between a gnome and a pixie. Her abundant silver hair circled a wrinkled face, yet bright eyes belied her age. "Miss Lila, you ready to draw the winning ticket?"

"That's what I'm here for," she responded tartly.

More chuckles rose from the crowd.

Without ceremony, Lila reached into the barrel. Her small glasses glinted in the light as she read the ticket. Then she handed it back to Steve. Squinting, he read it aloud. "The winner is Andrea McKenzie."

A murmur of surprise moved through the crowd at the unfamiliar name. But no one was more surprised than Andrea. "Me?" she squeaked.

"Cool," said one of the boys who stood close to her.

Andrea glanced at Jake and Brynn, then smiled tentatively. With the other teens encouraging her, she walked up to the front.

Brynn held her breath, wanting so much for this to be a good moment for Andrea.

"Congratulations, young lady." Peterson shook her hand, and was rewarded with a shy grin. "Your prize is crated up out back."

"Thank you."

Brynn and Jake flanked Andrea as she ac-

cepted good wishes from people she hadn't
even met.

When the music started up again, everyone
dispersed, couples gliding back into step, women
resuming their gossip, children chasing each
other across the cavernous barn.

"What do you suppose is 'crated up'?" Jake
whispered.

Brynn didn't hide her amusement. "I can't
even guess. But I'm hoping that if it fits in a
crate it can't be too large."

Andrea turned toward them, her face expectant. "I want to go see what I won."

Once outside, they stared in surprise at the
crate.

"I'd have never guessed this," Jake muttered.

"Me neither," Brynn agreed.

"They're great, aren't they?" Andrea asked
in awe.

"Yes," Jake admitted.

A peacock and peahen stared back at them.
Although the male's trademark tail plumes
weren't spread, his beautiful coloring still over-
shadowed that of his mate's.

Brynn cleared her throat. "They'll make quite
an addition to the ranch."

"Wow. My own peacocks," Andrea murmured.

As Jake met Brynn's gaze he realized they were sharing a different sort of moment. Brynn's eyes were clear, not clouded with pain or memories.

And it hit him.

He wanted to keep her that way—warm, unwounded, unguarded.

CHAPTER NINE

BRYNN SHARED THE NEWS of Andrea's unlikely win with Julia, checking to see if the peacock and hen would be welcome at her ranch. Delighted for the child, Julia agreed, suggesting they use the henhouse that had been empty for years. And, in a typical Julia gesture, she shipped a dozen red-plumed French chickens to keep the new couple company.

Brynn also confided that she had enjoyed the dance more than she'd thought possible. The resurgence of freedom was exhilarating. With Jake at her side, much of her confidence was returning. It was difficult to be afraid next to a strong man like him.

Andrea was also feeling freer and growing more confident. And in the days following the dance, she took charge of her small brood. The peacock and peahen settled in well. Accustomed to the ducks in the pond, the dogs didn't bother any of the birds. So Shamus still shadowed Andrea everywhere. Their bond was growing so deep that Brynn hoped Jake would agree to keep the duo together when they left. She wasn't quite so sure about what they'd do about the exotic birds. Andrea could have visitation rights, Brynn thought with a smile. But then she considered Jake and Andrea leaving, and the prospect left her stomach lurching.

Both of them had gotten to her, in such different ways. Andrea had thawed her numbed heart, and Jake…well…

She watched him now as he loaded the SUV, noting the symmetry of his body as all his muscles flowed together effortlessly. He did more for a pair of blue jeans and boots than ought to be legal.

"Are you sure the birds will be all right while we're gone?" Andrea fretted.

Brynn smiled. "We're going to the other side of the ranch for a picnic lunch, sweetie. We're not crossing the Alps."

"But this is still a new house for them. The chickens just got here last week."

"It was new to you, too," Brynn reminded her gently, tugging on her ponytail. "And look how well you're doing."

Andrea nodded, then hugged her quickly before scampering to the car. Glancing up, Brynn saw that Jake had seen the spontaneous gesture. But he didn't comment, instead opening the rear door so that the dogs could all jump inside. Then he drove to the picnic spot they all liked.

Andrea ate a small portion of pasta salad and half a banana. Afterward, she picked up the stick she'd taken to carrying when walking. "I'm going to find the dogs." Her newfound energy kicking in, she ran after the dogs, who were barking in pursuit of some invisible prey. Even Shamus had left her side to join the chase.

"Penny for your thoughts."

Brynn met Jake's gaze. "They're worth at least a nickel." She fiddled with her can of Diet Coke. "I'm very pleased with Andrea's progress."

He crossed long, lean legs. "I see it, too."

"She was so fragile...." Brynn felt the catch in her throat and tried to keep the hitch from her voice. "But now..."

"Yeah." His gaze touched hers. "Because of you."

Denial seemed inappropriate, a false modesty that had no place in a case as serious as Andrea's. "Hmm."

He plucked at the grass beside the quilt. "Do you have a better sense of how long you'll need to work with her?"

Brynn felt the blow as intensely as if the air had been physically knocked from her. "Well…I don't know. Her progress has astounded me. Um…is your leave of absence nearly up?"

"It's as long or short as I make it."

The painful subject of his job hadn't been broached since its last disastrous outing. Brynn knew Jake would have to face the truth at some point. And if she didn't push him to confront the decision, she wouldn't be helping him or his daughter.

In the distance Brynn heard the dogs bark. The sound was growing dim. Maternal instincts kicking in, she turned her head, listening more closely. "Do the dogs seem farther away to you?"

The two of them scrambled to their feet.

"Andrea!" Jake called, heading down the slope.

At his side, Brynn felt that horrible clutch that had stayed with her after Sarah's death. "Let's hurry!"

Jake didn't argue, and they jogged as quickly

as the tangling grass, rutted ground and rocks allowed. Looking down toward the level ground below, Jake saw no trace of Andrea or the dogs. As his gaze swept the area, he grabbed Brynn's hand, slowing her progress. "Listen. Don't you hear an echo?"

Panting, Brynn turned her head in the same direction. "You're right. It sounds faintly like the dogs—as though they're in a tunnel."

"Or a cave," Jake guessed.

Brynn gasped.

"They have to be close or we couldn't hear them," Jake reasoned, hoping his daughter hadn't done something foolish.

Following the dim sound of barking, Jake watched for an opening in the side of the hill. It wouldn't have to be large, he knew. Just big enough for a slim child and a large dog to enter.

They walked to an outcrop that ended in a steep ledge. Knowing it couldn't be the entrance, Jake turned. But Brynn didn't. Face pale, she stared over the edge.

"Brynn!" Impatient, he tried to hurry her.

When she didn't move, he turned back, catching her hand. Despite the warm day, her fingers were cold. And her expression didn't change.

"What is it?" He grasped her upper arms. "Brynn! We need to find—"

"Sarah."

"Brynn! Snap out of it!"

She crumpled a fraction. "Of course."

He didn't like the way she looked. "Why don't you stay here. I'll go find—"

"No! I'm okay. Let's find Andrea."

There wasn't time for a debate. But he held her hand as they reversed direction. Spotting a clump of tall bushes, he paused.

"I don't hear the dogs anymore!" Her voice was panicked.

"Me neither. Let's hope this is the entrance." Dropping Brynn's hand, Jake pushed through a slim break in the shrubbery.

"It's so dark," she whispered.

Jake thought of his child, frightened, alone, possibly hurt. Hand-in-hand, they walked into the cave, the darkness deepening, cautiously picking their way.

"Listen," Brynn whispered urgently.

He did. And far away he could hear a dog barking.

"That's Virgil."

Knowing how protective the dog was, Jake tightened his grip on Brynn's hand. If something had happened to Andrea, Virgil and Shamus would be the ones guarding her.

Cursing silently, Jake wished he had a flashlight. Luckily, the narrow walls allowed him to feel his way along. Moving forward a bit more quickly, he stumbled. Brynn reacted promptly, reaching for him as they steadied themselves against the wall.

He slowed down marginally, his heart still in his throat, imagining the worst. The passageway gradually widened and the blackness lifted slightly. As they pushed ahead, the barking sounded very close.

Then, as the passageway opened into a large cavern, it grew much lighter. Glancing up, Jake saw a hole in the roof of the cave that was allowing sunlight inside.

Jake stopped suddenly.

"Daddy!" Andrea stood against one wall, clearly terrified, her walking stick clutched in one hand.

And he could see why. The dogs had cornered a badger. Virgil and Shamus stood between the animal and Andrea, protecting her. But it was a standoff that could soon turn ugly.

The badger's teeth were bared and his deadly claws were ready to rip into man and beast.

Jake forced his voice to remain calm. "Annie, stay close to the wall and walk toward us slowly."

She took a step outward rather than to the side.

"No, Annie. Hug the wall."

Sinking back, she did as he instructed.

"Slowly, Annie."

She met his eyes, and although her lips wobbled, she obeyed.

It seemed to take forever, but finally she was beside them. Next to him, Brynn pulled Andrea close, stroking her hair, hugging her tightly. "Oh, Annie. We were so worried!"

Andrea's whimpers were muffled in Brynn's embrace as she clung to her. His throat tight, Jake watched them with relief, then bent to pick up the discarded walking stick. "Brynn, can you guide Annie back outside?"

"Yes, of course."

"All right, you two get going."

Brynn looked at him in concern. "What about you?"

"I'll be fine. Just take care of Andrea."

Though appearing torn, she nodded and left with his daughter.

Jake glanced at his watch, calculating how

long it would take them to get safely out to the entrance. Then he filled his pockets with several rocks of various sizes. As the minutes ticked by, he watched the badger, wondering if it would attack before he could get them all out of the cave.

When he was sure enough time had passed, he called Molly and Duncan to his side. They were reluctant, but not as determined to stay in the fight as the larger dogs. Then he had to decide which dog to call next. Both Virgil and Shamus had shown extraordinary protective instincts. But of the two, he felt Virgil might be the smarter. Hoping he was right, Jake called Shamus. The big dog clearly didn't want to come, so Jake sharpened his voice. Still barking at the badger, Shamus retreated.

With only Virgil threatening him, the badger continued the standoff, each animal looking ready to rip the other apart.

Jake called Virgil, but the dog continued growling, keeping the badger at bay.

"Virgil, come!"

Precious minutes passed before the dog acknowledged Jake. Still growling, he backed away.

Jake gripped the stick in one hand and a large

rock in the other. With Virgil close, he looked into the dog's eyes. "Find Brynn!" he commanded. "Now!"

Virgil hesitated, then took off down the tunnel, the other dogs following him as Jake had hoped.

Not wanting to turn his back on the badger, he edged out of the cave, hoping he wouldn't have to use the rocks. The badger remained against the far wall, every tooth and claw bared. It seemed to take forever, but Jake finally made it to the end of the passage. Blinking against the light, he pushed past the bushes.

"Daddy!"

"Jake!"

Twin voices of relief assaulted him before Andrea and Brynn nearly knocked him over with their hugs.

He squeezed Andrea tightly, making sure she wasn't harmed. "Are you really okay?"

She nodded. "I'm sorry, Daddy."

"I know. Next time maybe you'll listen to me about following the dogs."

"Yes. I didn't know what was going to happen."

Brynn had stepped back, but he could still feel

the warmth of her sudden embrace. She met his eyes. "We were so worried about you."

Feeling equally impulsive, he drew her close, kissing her fiercely. Before she could react, he looked back at the cave. "Let's get out of here. I don't know much about badgers, but he could be headed our way."

They hurried back to their picnic, packing everything in record time. Adrenaline pumping, Jake shared one more question-filled glance with Brynn.

THE HOUSE WAS QUIET. Dinner dishes were done. An exhausted Andrea had gone to bed, after giving both Jake and Brynn grateful hugs.

Retreating to the den, Jake poured a drink and settled into one of the aged leather chairs. The solidity of the sturdy furniture and the soothing yellow light cast by the lamps made the room seem a safe haven from the day's danger. Yet Jake couldn't relax.

He reached for one of the pictures on the side table—a photo of Brynn's daughter. He guessed that Brynn's secrets had something to do with Sarah. Studying the print, he saw a bright-eyed girl who resembled her mother. No mystery in her expression, nothing to suggest she'd been anything other than an ordinary preteen.

Hearing Brynn's light tread, he glanced up, seeing her smooth some lotion on her hands.

She chose the chair closest to his. "Annie's asleep."

"Good."

Brynn focused on the picture he held.

Jake, too, turned his eyes to the photo. "She was a lovely child."

Brynn nodded. "Very much so."

"Can you tell me about her?"

"I thought I had." Brynn's voice softened. "Sarah was a joy, a gift."

"And?"

Puzzled, she cocked her head. "And?"

"How did she die?"

Her face went still and she closed her eyes. When she opened them a few moments later, the pain was back. "In a fall."

He thought of the outcrop, the ledge they'd stood on that afternoon. "Here on the ranch?"

"No. Closer to home."

Jake also remembered how paralyzed Brynn had been. "I see why you were frightened today. You thought Andrea might repeat Sarah's accident."

Brynn glanced down, not meeting his gaze. "What is it?"

She twisted her hands. "Sarah's death wasn't an accident."

"What else could it be? A fall..." Then it hit him. Hard. "Suicide?"

Miserably, she nodded. "I didn't believe it at first. I was certain it was an accident. My Sarah wouldn't, couldn't want to kill herself. The day it...happened I was supposed to go hiking with Sarah and her friend Michelle. I begged off— I just didn't feel like going. It was the same apathy I'd had since Kirk's death. But I thought it was safe for the girls to go together. They'd been hiking since they were very young. But then Michelle couldn't go, leaving Sarah on her own."

Brynn bent her head again. "When the sheriff told me that Sarah was dead, I remember screaming, then demanding to see her." She bit her trembling lips. "Her body was so broken.... I didn't think anything worse could ever happen. Then, a few days later, the coroner ruled her death a suicide. He cited Kirk's death, Sarah's failing grades, inattentiveness, depression, all marks of suicide." Brynn's agony was palpable. "I refused to believe it. No one knew my Sarah like I did. I couldn't believe she would take the

life I'd given her. But my family said they'd
seen all the classic signs of suicide, everything
that came out at the inquest. They told me I was
in denial, that I refused to see the truth. I hadn't
taken their warnings seriously because I thought
they were overreacting.''

Brynn's voice caught. ''I hated to accept that
my own child had been unbearably depressed.
She was sad, of course, but not more than I
would have expected. She was always there for
me after Kirk's death—accepting much of the
responsibility that should have been mine. But
at her age, it was just too much. Losing her father, then having to prop up her mother, well…
I should have looked after her. It was my job,
my sacred trust.''

''You can't believe her death was your fault.''

''I failed her.''

''I don't believe that.''

''Believe it.'' Brynn's voice was dull.
''Sarah's dead. And I didn't protect her.''

''We can't be there every minute.'' Jake
thought about Brynn's concerns involving his
job. Was she projecting her own fears onto him?
''As much as I love Andrea, I don't want to
watch her constantly. Suffocating her that way
wouldn't help either of us.''

Brynn lifted her head, her expression one of quiet dignity. ''No. But apathy is a terrible thing. So is self-absorption.''

''Brynn Alder, you are the least self-absorbed person I've ever met!''

''You didn't know me then. All I could think about was losing Kirk.''

''Just for yourself?''

''Well...for Sarah, too. Still—''

''You're generous, kind, compassionate. You can't convince me that you've had a drastic Jekyll and Hyde transformation since Sarah died.''

Brynn met his eyes, her own tortured. ''Maybe not Jekyll and Hyde, but the fact remains that Sarah's gone. And nothing will ever bring her back.''

Jake took her hands, warming them in his own. He didn't know why Sarah had died, but his knowledge of Brynn was sure. And her pain was a knife to his heart. A heart that had opened only for her.

CHAPTER TEN

THE WORD *PICNIC* HADN'T had good connotations since the cave incident, but an organized town picnic was different.

As Andrea hung out with the kids she'd met at the dance, Brynn was glad they'd decided to come. It had been a rough week. Jake had stirred her pain, brought it all to the surface again. But the process had brought an unexpected change. She found that she was no longer comparing Andrea to Sarah.

Her feelings for Andrea weren't an extension of those for Sarah. Instead, she saw more differences than similarities. Yet her love for Andrea continued to grow. She knew it would hurt terribly when the child and her father left, but Brynn couldn't stop the feelings.

And the old-fashioned picnic was a delight. She hadn't known such traditions still existed. But then she supposed that people in small towns had to develop their own social calendars.

It was a perfect day, warm with a light breeze that carried the scent of freshly mown grass. Tables had been set up beneath tall oak trees, but plenty of people chose to recline on bright quilts that dotted the field.

There were activities for everyone, young and old. Brynn and Jake decided to forgo apple dunking, but Mary Bainter kept urging them to join in some of the other games.

Shouts rose from across the field.

"The sack race," Jake muttered.

"That's something you could do with Andrea," Brynn suggested.

His expression grew speculative. "Or you."

"Me?"

"Mary's insisting that we join in."

"In the three-legged sack race?"

Jake took her hand. And before she could protest, he was tugging her toward the group.

When he took a sack from the pile, she groaned. "Don't tell me we're really going to do this!"

He fitted the sack around two of their legs. "Yep."

Then his arm was around her waist, hers around his. They hopped, jiggled, wiggled, stumbled, gasped, giggled and squawked their way toward the finish line. Falling into each other, then grabbing arms, hands and torsos to stay upright, they escaped the seriousness of the past days.

A few feet from the finish line they couldn't avoid a final tumble, flopping forward on the grass.

Laughing helplessly, Brynn stretched out one hand. "I think I touched the line."

Jake met her gaze, his own eyes filled with happiness. "Since we were in about tenth place I don't think that means we win."

The sun was warm, but Brynn doubted that was the cause of the heat she felt. Was that wonder she glimpsed in Jake's face?

The sound of clapping and shouting made her glance up. She saw the winners celebrating. Then she looked back at Jake. Swallowing, she wondered how the moment would have developed if they weren't surrounded by people.

Jake pushed the sack from their legs, then reached for her hand. Standing upright, Brynn found her feelings were still out of whack.

But there was Andrea to consider, so Brynn concentrated on everything except the way she'd felt in Jake's arms. Yet the warmth stayed with her, buoyed her as the day drew to a close and they traveled back to the ranch.

As they parked, she could hear the dogs barking. Strange, they didn't usually make such a fuss. Of course, they weren't that fond of being shut in the barn. But she hadn't wanted to leave them with the cats in the house. The animals usually got along well, but a whole day locked up together could fray the best canine dispositions.

When she unlatched the barn door, the dogs rushed toward her. Molly and Duncan scratched at her knees, while Shamus barked, then ran outside to find Andrea. But Virgil looked at her with such entreaty that she knelt down. "What is it, boy?"

His tail didn't swish in its usual greeting.

She ran a hand over his mane.

"Anything wrong?" Jake asked from behind.

She stood. "Not really. Virgil's just acting strange."

"Maybe he's hungry. I know I am."

Brynn smiled. "All males have a healthy appetite." As she walked out of the barn, Virgil ran ahead to the house. Jake glanced toward his retreating body. "He seems okay now."

She decided he was right. "He probably didn't like being cooped up."

"I'll check out the barn, make sure everything's okay."

Leaving him, Brynn headed into the house. Humming beneath her breath, she decided it was nice to have a man around. Once in the kitchen,

Brynn reached for her apron. As she tied the strings, she glanced through the window. The blind was closed. Funny, she thought she'd left it up.

Deciding that Jake or Andrea must have lowered it, she forgot about the blind. The supper she planned was simple, but they'd had a large lunch at the picnic. She smiled. It was almost difficult to believe she'd cut herself off from so much since moving to the ranch. Remarkably, Jake made her feel safe.

And that was something she'd despaired of ever being again.

ALTHOUGH THE RANCH wasn't huge, the rolling landscape seemed to be endless. Jake leaned forward as Fortune galloped toward the creek. They'd had a long ride and both were ready for a break.

The creek wasn't deep. Although this part of the country was susceptible to flash floods, the weather had been dry. As Fortune drank from the stream, Jake squatted beside him, cupping his hand to collect some of the clear, cool water. The only sounds he could hear were those of the burble of the creek and the hum of insects.

He hadn't really ever considered the silence of rural life. The quiet that Brynn encouraged allowed him to think without distraction. Although the peace was intended to help troubled kids to heal, it had become an unexpected balm for him as well.

And in the past few days, he'd been thinking about Brynn's daughter. He had probed a bit further and learned that the two had practically been inseparable, a true case of mother and daughter being friends. And the girl had been there for Brynn during the tragedy of Kirk's death, the pair growing even closer.

So why would Sarah commit suicide?

She was young, but not too young to understand the devastating effects of such an action on Brynn. It didn't make sense.

Fortune snorted.

Jake glanced in the water one last time, but saw only his reflection, not the answers he wanted. He stood. "Okay, boy." He swung his leg over the horse, then settled in the saddle. He could ride back the way he'd come or take the shortcut. Wanting, needing to talk to Brynn again, he chose the latter.

Fortune could have ridden for hours more, but he accepted Jake's firm hand and headed home. Back at the barn, as Jake unsaddled the stallion, he thought of his father. His financial success had provided riding lessons for Jake. And piano lessons, judo, whatever he wanted. There had never been a debate on whether the luxuries were needed. Harold McKenzie's focus on career left little time for debate. Or for his son.

Jake remembered his now ironic and superior notion that he would do better, and sighed heavily. How had he been so blind to his own failure until now? Absently he patted Fortune's mane, then reached for a brush.

When had he last visited his father other than for a duty call? Longer than he could remember. If he had, perhaps Andrea would be closer to her grandfather. Maybe now that Jake's dad was retired, he could have filled some of the gaps in her life.

The phone in the barn rang and Jake stopped brushing. Glancing at the phone, he realized it was the first time it had rung since he'd been there. Brynn used a cell phone and the house phone virtually never rang. Strange.

Finishing up with Fortune, he left the barn. He entered the house through the back door, but the kitchen was empty. Poking his head in the studio, he saw Andrea there, but not Brynn. He finally spotted her in the door. She was standing by the telephone, lost in thought.

"Brynn?"

"Hmm?" She looked up, clearly distracted. "Oh, hello."

"Something wrong?"

"What?"

He pointed to the telephone. "Bad news?"

"No...no. Whoever it was hung up when I answered."

Not before she reached the phone, but after she answered. "That's odd."

She didn't reply.

"Don't you think so?"

Brynn touched the phone, then turned away from it. "I used to get calls like this just after Kirk died."

Jake's instincts kicked in. "And?"

She shrugged. "I never learned why."

"But you had your suspicions."

Her head flew up, her expression startled. "What makes you say that?"

"Brynn, it makes sense. You live out in the middle of nowhere, you panic whenever your routine is disrupted. Something drove you here. What was it?"

She held his gaze for so long he wondered if she would answer. Then she glanced down. "After Kirk died I had a lot of these calls. I'd answer. No one would speak."

"Did you report them to the police?"

"Not until after the break-in." She took a deep breath. "It was the day of Kirk's funeral."

He winced.

"The police told me it wasn't uncommon—criminals watch the obituaries, then rob the house during the services." She paused, more pain filling her eyes. "But I wasn't thinking very clearly then…and I didn't realize that while the house was ransacked, nothing much of value was taken except Kirk's cameras."

"Cameras?"

She pushed one hand through her thick hair. "Yes. He was a photographer. Anyway, after the break-in the calls continued. And then one day when I came home, I was sure someone had been in the house again. It wasn't as blatant that time, but I could tell."

Jake felt the icy premonition of danger. "Did you call the police?"

Brynn nodded. "They took my concerns seriously. Only…" She bit her lower lip.

"What is it?"

"They asked if Kirk could have been connected to something illegal."

He could tell she refused to believe that was possible.

"So I agreed to let them search the house, including his studio. They didn't find anything. They also examined the photos that were in archival storage.''

"What about his current photos?"

"They were stolen during the first break-in."

Jake frowned. "Didn't the cops find that odd?"

"Yes. And because they did, it jogged my memory, which still wasn't in good shape at the time. I told them that the cameras Kirk always carried in his car weren't there after the crash. But I couldn't be sure what had happened to them. They could have been stolen by the wrecker, or at the junkyard.... It wasn't something we could pinpoint."

"So the police dropped the case?"

"Not exactly. They spent a great deal of time examining every photo, but couldn't find anything that pointed to a connection."

"And the phone calls?"

"The police said they were from a nontraceable cell phone."

Which could have meant kids playing a prank, or something far more menacing.

"That brought them to a dead end. But I was fearful for Sarah's safety. I couldn't be sure the people wouldn't try again, maybe when we were home. So I moved. I hoped that whatever they wanted would be forgotten once we disappeared.''

"And?''

She chewed her lip again. "For a while that seemed to be true. But then Sarah died.''

Instinctively, Jake reached for Brynn's hand.

She swallowed past the pain. "After she was… gone, I didn't care what happened to me. But when the second house was broken in to, my family insisted that I move again. Knowing how it felt to lose a daughter, I couldn't do the same thing to my own mother. And Julia was certain I'd be safe here at the ranch.''

"Any odd things happen here?''

She met his eyes. "Only when you showed up at my door.''

She must have been terrified. His hand still over hers, he pulled her close. "I'm sorry for that.''

Brynn resisted for a moment before accepting his embrace. "If you hadn't…well, you wouldn't be here now.''

Holding her, he digested the words. As the moments passed, he glanced down at the innocent-looking telephone and prayed it wasn't about to announce more trouble.

CHAPTER ELEVEN

IT WAS LATE. And Brynn was tired. Confiding in Jake had been somewhat therapeutic, but also emotionally exhausting. Now, watching Andrea as she slept, Brynn felt her heart tighten. She had grown so close to this child. Every new smile, the slightest improvement, etched itself on her soul. No matter what the future brought, she would have this memory to hold close.

A rustling at the door made her look up. The dim light from the hallway outlined Jake's tall figure. Bending down, she lightly kissed Andrea's forehead, then withdrew.

Jake's voice was hushed. ''Are you okay?''

Hating to see the worry she'd caused in his eyes, she smiled. ''Yes. It's comforting to watch Andrea sleep, to know she's safe, nearly well.''

His hand came up to her cheek. ''I've opened a bottle of wine. Will you join me?''

She warmed beneath his touch and battled the

urge to lean into the embrace, sensing it would lead to far more than comfort.

"Yes."

They walked down the wide staircase side by side. In the den, she saw that Jake had lit a fire, perfect for the cool night.

He poured the wine and brought both glasses across the room, handing her one. Sitting beside her, he stretched out his legs, propping his feet on the slightly scarred, heavy oak coffee table that seemed made for that very purpose.

"I've thought a lot about my father today."

His words surprised her. He'd never talked about his family before. Then it hit her: he was trying to distract her. "Any special reason?"

"Yeah. It took me long enough, but I finally realized that I've been following my father's example."

"I imagine we all do that to some extent."

He shook his head. "Not like I have. I'm repeating every mistake he made."

"Has this been a recent revelation?"

"Afraid so." He twirled the glass back and forth slowly. "And I probably wouldn't have realized it if I hadn't failed so badly with Andrea."

Feeling his pain, Brynn laid her hand on his

arm. "You're judging yourself too harshly. You couldn't prevent your ex-wife from leaving, for how that affected Annie."

"I spent too much time away from Andrea, expecting a child to deal with a woman I didn't want to face anymore."

"But you have the future to remedy that," Brynn reminded him gently.

He sighed. "Yeah. And I wish I could say it won't bother me to resign or take a lesser position, but it will. So what kind of father does that make me?"

Putting her glass on the table, she turned toward him. "One who's human, who loves his daughter. When we met you wouldn't have even considered a career change."

"I suppose not. You have a way about you, Brynn."

She tightened her grip on his arm. "So do you."

With the words, the air between them seemed to shift, the room becoming heavy with expectation.

With his free hand, Jake tucked her hair behind one ear. A second later he put his wineglass on the table. This time when their lips met, there was room for discovery.

Brynn felt him unlock something inside her, evoking sensations that made her breath catch. As he had before, Jake reminded her that she was still a woman, one with needs, even desires. She made no comparisons. Jake wasn't a replacement for her late husband. He was an original.

Confidence pushed him, she knew. She felt it in his touch. But a deeper emotion gentled him now. And, forgetting the yesterdays, the qualms, the pain, she allowed new sensations to absorb her.

One of his hands traced over her neck, pausing at her throat, then moving to her breast.

She tilted her head back a fraction, unable to stop the gasp he caused. It had been so long. And the newness of his touch, like that of a first kiss, made her quake with anticipation. And when he brought his hand back to her face, she felt a sharp disappointment.

His eyes were dark, she realized after a moment, after she could focus. Dark with the same need she was feeling?

His deep voice, now slightly husky, grabbed her attention, and she noticed his chest heaving with uneven breaths. "I'm not about to take advantage of your emotional state, Brynn. When I make love to you, it's going to be when you can think clearly, remember every word, every gesture.''

She met his gaze, reading a promise that caused her to tremble.

''Tonight I only want to take your mind off the day.''

Her smile was shaky. ''That you've done.''

His mouth came dangerously close to hers again. ''I need to get my head straight. And this near to you, it's not going to happen.''

Unable to resist, she pressed her lips against his once more. ''Then I'll say good night.''

Disappointment and desire darkened his eyes even more, and as she crossed the room, Brynn felt his gaze as strongly as though his arms still surrounded her. That was a good thing, she decided. A very good thing.

A FEW AFTERNOONS later they walked toward the house, returning from a hike. Andrea led the trio, again using the stick she always carried when outside.

The dogs happily ran alongside, chasing everything from butterflies to the bits of fluff that drifted from nearby cottonwood trees. But they didn't wander away.

Jake didn't expect to repeat the cave experience, but he preferred to be cautious. Safety was on his mind more than ever before.

The house was close now, so he took the lead. Not wanting to frighten Andrea, he had decided to say nothing to her about Brynn's fears. As they neared the stable, everything looked calm, the same as they'd left it.

"I want to check on the horses," Andrea announced, turning away from them. Shamus was at her heels.

"Why don't you go with Andrea?" Jake suggested, once his daughter was out of earshot. "See how Fortune and Destiny are doing."

Brynn looked at him strangely. "If something's wrong in the house, I want to be there."

Damn. He hadn't wanted to worry her. "I didn't know I was that transparent."

"I've been living with this for a while now."

The back door was unlocked, as they'd left it. Jake had wrestled over that detail, finally deciding that it was better to act normally. If Roy needed to enter the house and the door was locked, it could set off an alarm they weren't yet ready to handle.

Jake checked out the kitchen, but didn't see anything out of place. "Look okay to you?"

Brynn nodded. "I think so."

The den was next. While Jake glanced around, Brynn walked to the desk, her expression changing.

"What is it?"

She lifted her shoulders in a small shrug. "I'm not sure. Probably nothing."

"Tell me."

"I thought I'd left the address book open, but I can't be sure."

It was a small thing. But was it a clue? "I'm going upstairs."

She nodded. "I'll check my room, too."

It didn't take long for Jake to go through his and Andrea's bedrooms. He didn't find anything amiss. Brynn emerged from her room, her expression noncommittal.

"Anything?"

Brynn shook her head slowly. "No."

But she didn't sound completely sure. "What is it?"

"Well…nothing really. Just a weird feeling." She met his eyes. "Do you know what I mean?"

"Yeah. Do you think it's because we've talked about the break-ins?"

"Could be. I haven't thought about it as much

since you've been here. Now it's out in the open.''

''Even the strongest people need help now and then.''

''You think I'm strong?'' she asked in surprise.

And brave. And beautiful. ''Yes.''

She didn't speak for a moment. ''Oh.''

Knowing Andrea could come into the house at any minute, he shelved the rest of his thoughts. But they stayed with him through dinner, then through several games of cards with his daughter and Brynn.

Finally Andrea was ready to go to bed. He returned her hug, then watched as she hugged Brynn just as naturally. Val hadn't been one for hugs. He saw that Brynn's gaze remained on Andrea as she climbed the stairs, until she disappeared.

''She's an absolute delight,'' Brynn murmured.

He'd always thought so, at least until her breakdown. ''Yes. But I don't mind a little adult time.''

''That's because Andrea wins all the games,'' she teased. Her gaze touched his, then fell away.

They were both conscious of the fact that they were alone together once more.

Jake cleared his throat. "Brynn, you told me about Kirk's photos, the ones the police examined. Do you have any of them here?"

"Yes. I brought along those that were taken out of the archives. Why?"

He hesitated, not wanting to share his doubts. "Would it bother you to go through them again?"

Her eyes sobered. "No. It's good to remember. I don't want to just forget him, as though he never existed. His memory deserves more."

What would it be like to be on the receiving end of that kind of love? Jake pondered that question as Brynn went to retrieve the photos. He refilled their coffee mugs, adding cream to hers, the way she preferred. Funny, the details he knew about her.

He stirred the coffee, unable to stop worrying. Brynn didn't seem to realize there had to be something in her possession that someone wanted badly.

It took her a while, but she finally returned and settled beside him on the couch, holding a bag of frozen spinach. "They're in here."

He lifted his eyebrows in surprise. "I'm guessing you took the spinach out first."

"This will sound silly, but after I moved here, I had a strange feeling about the pictures. So I put them out of sight in the walk-in freezer." As she spoke, she unsealed the Ziploc bag she'd removed from the spinach bag, then withdrew some of the pictures, spreading them on the coffee table.

They were brilliant, Jake realized. He hadn't expected anything of this caliber. He knew enough about photography to recognize the man's talent. Someone this gifted, married to a fine woman like Brynn...surely he hadn't turned to something illegal! "Was Kirk successful?"

"Very much so. The critics loved even his earliest work. He was known for capturing something elusive in his images, almost another dimension. They called him a genius."

And why would a genius risk everything? Jake carefully studied a small stack of photos, impressed a bit more with each one.

"His shows were incredible," she recalled.

"I can see why."

She lightly touched the edge of one photo. "But do you see anything else?"

He felt her pain. She desperately wanted to

disprove the authorities' suspicions. She didn't want to believe her late husband was someone she should have distrusted. "No. Why don't we go through them slowly? Together? Maybe one of us will nudge the other's thoughts, see something that's not obvious."

An hour ticked by, then another. But as they studied the pictures, Jake found it difficult to remain detached. Like Brynn, her late husband had been an artist. Was this the bond that had held them so close?

Knowing he didn't possess a single artistic bone, Jake felt the differences between them mounting. Kirk had been a dedicated family man, as well. Another strike for Jake.

Brynn sighed. "I've done this a dozen times before and I still don't see anything."

He wasn't ready to give up that quickly. "Perhaps it's so subtle…"

"That no one can find it?" she suggested in a discouraged voice. "It's not that I don't want to see something if it's genuinely there, but after the detectives, then the police labs…well, it's difficult to believe everyone missed even a single clue."

But what else could Brynn have that someone wanted so desperately?

Jake glanced toward the staircase, thinking of his sleeping daughter. If Brynn was still in danger, he might be risking Andrea's safety by staying here. Yet, if he took her away, Andrea's recovery could backslide.

Shifting his gaze to Brynn, Jake wasn't certain he could leave anyway.

CHAPTER TWELVE

ANDREA WAS QUIET. Quieter than she had been
in weeks. Jake's first instinct was to go to the
studio and ask Brynn to speak with his daughter.
His daughter. If he couldn't talk to Andrea
now, what had he learned since coming here?
Swallowing, he thought of his own father. "Annie, is something wrong?"

"Not exactly."

"Then what is it, exactly?"

"Well...I got this phone call."

Adrenaline blocked out everything else. "A
crank call?"

"No. It was Todd."

Confused, he narrowed his eyes. "Todd?"

"I met him at the dance, then I saw him again
at the picnic."

"Oh." A new concern pushed away the first
one.

"Well, he sorta asked if I wanted to go on
the hayride."

Jake frowned. "You're not old enough to go on a date."

Andrea sighed. "It wouldn't be a date. It's just a bunch of kids going together."

He still didn't like it. "How old is this Todd?"

"Daddy!" she said reproachfully. "He's thirteen."

Hardly an older man, but Andrea was his baby. "I don't know."

"How come?"

Because she was already growing up too fast. Because he didn't want her to get hurt, to learn any of life's hard lessons. "When's the hayride?"

"Tonight. Todd's dad is going to drive the wagon."

"I see." Feeling hopelessly inept, Jake stalled. "I'll think about it."

"You can't think very long. I need to call Todd back."

It was difficult to reconcile her logic with his own fear. "Okay."

She jumped up. "I think Roy's here."

"Head on outside. I'll find you."

But it was Brynn he needed to find, to talk to. Luckily, she was still in the studio.

She stopped working, wiping her hands on a towel and listening to him talk as he paced. "What's your first instinct?" she finally asked.

"Panic. Followed by a strong desire to lock Andrea in her room until she's about thirty-five."

She smiled. "Was there a third option?"

"Does there have to be?" He slowed his pacing, then sighed. "I was totally unprepared for this."

"Who isn't?" She paused. "So, it's a group activity."

"Yeah. With this Todd kid."

Her lips twitched. "You manage to make the boy sound like a cross between Freddy Krueger and the slickest bad boy on the planet."

"I don't know anything about him!"

"Maybe we can change that. You can talk to Roy, ask about the boy, his family. And I'll call Julia, see if she can add anything else."

Jake stared at her. "I hadn't thought of that."

"It will be easier to make a decision when you have more information."

He frowned. "Funny. In a work situation I would have seen that."

Brynn met his gaze. "You don't love your

work as much as you love Andrea. And that tends to send good sense out the window.''

He noted the caring in her eyes. How was he going to handle Andrea without this intelligent woman? ''Yet you knew what to do.''

''Parenting is easier in pairs. And this got thrown at you without warning. Once you'd had time to think, you would have figured out what to do.''

''That's highly debatable. Thanks, Brynn.''

She pushed the hair from her face, tucking it behind one ear, making him wish he'd thought of doing it for her. ''Sure. Um, I guess I'll call Julia,'' Brynn added when he didn't speak.

Realizing he was still staring, Jake stepped back. ''I'll see if Roy's outside.''

Brynn nodded. ''We can compare surveillance results in a few minutes.''

Unexpectedly, he smiled.

''That's better. You looked positively grim before.''

It hit him that she was the light he'd never before realized was missing in his life. Despite all of her private pain, Brynn made him smile. That she could struck him as incredible.

Finding a distraction for Andrea in the barn, Jake got the lowdown from Roy. It seemed Todd

Jenkins and his family were well thought of in the community. Todd had never been in any trouble, other than the usual childish pranks. His worst crime was once putting laundry detergent in the fountain in the town square.

Julia seconded the recommendation, adding that the boy was bright, had spirit. And that Andrea should be very safe on the hayride, a traditional Walburg event.

So Jake reluctantly said yes. But he insisted on driving Andrea to town and then returning later to pick her up.

Andrea was thrilled. After hugging her father, she begged Brynn to help her choose what to wear. Brynn suggested jeans because of the scratchy straw that would line the wagon. But it took nearly an hour to settle on which top she preferred.

Brynn glanced over Andrea's shoulder into the tall mirror. "You look lovely in everything."

Andrea met her eyes in the mirror. "You always say that."

Smiling, Brynn nodded. "I suppose I do. Lovely begins on the inside, Annie. And you've got everyone beat on that score."

Andrea glanced down.

Concerned, Brynn gently turned the girl around. "What is it, sweetie?"

"I want to stay here, Brynn, not go back to the city."

Her heart filled with love for this precious child. But Andrea belonged to Jake. Swallowing, Brynn tried to stem the emotion clogging her throat. "I can't think of anything I'd like more. But your father's going to have to get back to work soon."

"Why can't he stay here?" Andrea protested.

Brynn pulled her close, trying to convey in her hug what words lacked. "It's not that simple, Annie. You and your father have a life in San Antonio. And…well…"

"He likes you, I can tell," Andrea argued. "And you like him."

Brynn wished it didn't have to be so complicated. And she couldn't help wondering why yet another child she couldn't keep had been brought into her life. A child whose father she wanted, as well. She couldn't voice either thought, so she rocked Andrea from side to side, the lulling action soothing her raw feelings.

When Andrea was calmer, Brynn helped do her hair, spending time brushing the soft waves. Sarah had always been too impatient to stand still for that. But Andrea was content to have Brynn brush her hair endlessly. It was something she usually did each day now, another special connection between them.

Andrea insisted on wearing the locket Brynn had given her, fussing as the time to leave grew close.

The phone rang more often than it ever had since Brynn had come to the ranch. Calls back and forth between Andrea and Todd, between Andrea and one of the girls in town. Even Mary Bainter phoned. Everyone wanted the night to be perfect for Andrea. It was a milestone in her recovery.

When it was time to drive into town, Brynn decided to ride along. Andrea let the dogs jump into the SUV, too. But the dogs were good travelers, so neither Brynn nor Jake protested.

The kids were meeting at the Jenkins' house, which was close to town. Armed with her dad's and Brynn's good wishes, Andrea joined the rest.

Norm Jenkins approached, extending his hand. "Good to see you. Don't worry about your girl. I'll keep an eye on her. I've got three of my own."

Jake felt relief as he shook the other man's hand. "Thanks. I'd appreciate that."

"No problem."

Other kids arrived, their parents dropping them off. Brynn touched Jake's arm. "I think we probably ought to leave. Andrea's going to feel strange if you're the only parent who stays around."

"Oh."

"I'll buy you an ice-cream cone in town," Brynn offered. "Guaranteed to put a smile on your face."

"I didn't realize I looked that woebegone."

"Afraid so."

He sighed. "I guess she's going to grow up no matter what I do. You're right, let's get out of here."

The dogs hung their heads out of the windows, tongues lolling happily as they drove into town.

At the small hamburger stand that also sold ice cream, he and Brynn each chose a vanilla cone and settled at one of the small, round tables outside.

A light breeze ruffled Brynn's hair and she laughed as she tried to keep it out of her ice cream. He loved the sound. Like her voice and her movements, her laughter was graceful, melodic.

It was quiet. Nothing stayed open late in Walburg. The only places still doing business were the grocery store, the diner and the hamburger stand.

Jake's gaze traveled down the quiet street. "It's hard to believe a place like this exists."

"Especially having come from the big city," Brynn agreed. "For Julia it's a retreat. A place to think, to regroup."

"What about you?"

She crumpled a paper napkin, then dabbed at a puddle of ice cream that had dripped on the table. "At first, it was just an escape. But lately…well, it's been better."

He met her gaze. So much remained unspoken. Burned by Val's actions, Jake didn't think he was ready for marriage again. But Brynn wasn't the kind of woman who would accept anything less.

Questions lingered in her eyes, but he talked instead about Andrea. They laughed over their own youthful escapades, gruesome first dates and the pitfalls of teenage love.

But they didn't broach the even more painful

topic of adult love. Briefly Jake wondered how it would have been had he met Brynn years ago. Would he have realized the value of family earlier, or would he have just made a mess of that relationship, too?

After taking the dogs for a long romp in the park, they collected Andrea at the Jenkins'. She talked nonstop on the way back to the ranch, detailing her entire evening, giving them a description of each of the kids on the hayride.

Jake caught Brynn's eye and they shared a smile. It seemed very natural, the three of them together. Just like a family.

Once at the house, Jake parked and Andrea immediately opened the tailgate for the dogs. Happy to be out of the vehicle, they ran off, with Andrea close behind.

Jake was ready for some coffee now. Opening the back door, he took the precaution of entering first. Everything looked okay. He turned to Brynn to say so, but her expression stopped him.

Face white, she stared at him, her eyes appearing huge against her pale complexion.

"What is it, Brynn?"

"The blind was open. I'm sure of it." She pointed to the African violet on the counter.

"The plant needed sun so I put it on the windowsill. It was the last thing I did before I left. You and Andrea were already outside."

"A neighbor could have stopped by."

"To move the African violet?"

"Were there any odd phone calls today?"

She went very still.

"Brynn?"

It took her a moment to speak. "The phone was ringing all day, more than it ever has since I moved here. Someone did hang up when I answered, but I thought it was a kid."

"Hey, who locked Bert and Ernie in the butler's pantry?" Andrea demanded, pushing open the swinging door between the kitchen and the dining room.

Brynn met Jake's gaze before speaking. "They've shut themselves into rooms before."

Bert skidded across the kitchen floor, his back arched.

"Well, they're sure pissed this time," Andrea replied. Even Ernie ignored his food, stalking past them. "I can put them in my room tonight, let them know we didn't do it on purpose."

"That's sweet, Annie." Brynn tried to sound normal. "They'd like that."

"Silly cats," Andrea chided them, then bent down to give each a cuddle.

"Would you round up the birds?" Brynn asked. "It's getting late."

"Okay."

After she left, Brynn turned to Jake. "You'll have to leave in the morning. Take Andrea and go where you're sure it's safe."

He grasped her arms. "And leave you here alone?"

"My safety isn't the issue. Andrea's is."

"Of course I want her to be safe. I want you both to be safe. At the moment all we know is that we had a couple of callers hang up and a plant's been moved."

"You're forgetting Bert and Ernie."

"You said yourself they've locked themselves away before."

"Yes, but—"

"If we're leaving, we're all going."

"I don't want you to go," Brynn admitted. "Either of you. But I care too much about Andrea to put her in danger."

"I won't let anything happen to her," Jake asserted. His hands tightened on her arms as he drew her close. "Or to you."

Doubt, hope and fear clashed in her eyes.

Remembering everything she'd told him, Jake valiantly hoped he would be able to keep that promise.

IN THE DAYS THAT FOLLOWED, Brynn was on edge, watching, listening, her nerves stretched taut. But the phone didn't ring, the African violet didn't move, and even Bert and Ernie managed to keep out of trouble.

Had she let her imagination run away with her? she wondered, as she tested the clay beneath her hands. She'd been so sure about the plant, but it had been a frantic day. She glanced over at Andrea, who was working on a special vase. Brynn's emotions were still wound up from the girl's touching words, her desire to remain at the ranch.

Both Brynn and Jake remained on alert. He didn't go to town alone anymore, not wanting to leave them on their own. And he had checked all the window and door locks. But it wasn't a house designed to repel intruders. The French doors that led to the terrace could easily be forced. Though she normally left them ajar most of the day, now Brynn checked them often when she was in her studio.

Her art remained a calming influence. With

Andrea beside her, the cool clay in her hands, Brynn could almost believe that everything was all right.

She glanced at the girl, so absorbed in the vase she was throwing. Andrea was nearly recovered. All that was left was to make sure her connection to her father remained strong, that he could somehow reconcile his career with her needs.

Brynn leaned forward, careful not to disturb Virgil. His head was pillowed by her feet as he slept. He'd been even more vigilant lately, no doubt picking up on her anxiety. Poor thing was probably exhausted. And Shamus, always ready for a nap, was stretched out beside Andrea.

Studying the clay, Brynn envisioned the piece she planned for Craven Galleries. Briefly she closed her eyes, feeling the clay with her fingers, then the inexplicable sensation flowing up over her hands and arms as the spark of inspiration traveled.

It sometimes surprised her, coming at a moment when she was certain she would be blocked by worry. It was a wonder, a bit of magic. And it fed her soul.

The minutes slipped effortlessly into hours. Distracted only by checking occasionally on Andrea, Brynn was totally absorbed in her work.

She heard the rumble in Virgil's chest at nearly the same moment she felt him jump up from her feet. Shamus joined in barking. A few moments later she heard a huge crash in the kitchen. Terrified, she jerked her head.

Andrea looked only mildly curious. "One of the cats probably got on the counter again."

Heart pounding, Brynn tried not to panic. "Stay here."

The girl shrugged. "Okay."

Brynn raced toward the kitchen, the dogs ahead of her. Pushing open the door, she was stunned to see Jake on the floor, Mary Bainter in a heap beside him. They were both plastered in red…and what appeared to be some kind of light brown dough.

"Jake? Mary?"

Mary uttered a nearly breathless chuckle. "This is probably going to be a great story someday."

"What happened?"

"Jake gave me a fright. The strudel and I went flying, I'm afraid."

"I didn't hear her call out," Jake explained, helping Mary to her feet. "I'm sorry, Mary. It startled me when the door opened."

"Obviously. You expecting a serial killer?"

Brynn met Jake's eyes. "Of course not. Jake's accustomed to living in the city. Someone opens the door there without warning and it could be a burglar."

Jake released Mary's arm. "Are you all right?"

"I am. Not sure I can say the same for the strudel."

Brynn reached for a towel. "I hope the berries won't stain your clothes."

"Not to worry. I'm wearing work duds." She accepted the towel, then glanced first at Jake, then Brynn. "What's going on?"

"Nothing," they replied in unison.

Brynn wished she hadn't spoken.

Mary glanced at them again. "Uh-huh. Well, if this nothing keeps up, or you need anything, we're not far."

Reaching for a mug, Brynn turned so that Mary couldn't see her face. "I insist on making you a cup of tea. It's good to settle the nerves."

"Then you might want to make that three cups," Mary suggested.

Jake grabbed some paper towels, trying to wipe up the mess before the dogs finished licking up the tasty disaster.

Once the teakettle was filled and on the stove, Brynn turned around. ''Sugar?''

Mary's eyes were filled with concern. ''No, thanks.''

''Cookies or...'' Brynn's voice trailed off at the sound of Jake stuffing the remains of the strudel into the trash.

The minutes that followed were equally awkward. After a tense cup of tea, Mary left.

Looking through the window, Brynn watched her leave, feeling completely drained. ''That was close.''

''I overreacted.''

She sighed. ''Maybe I have been, too. It's not as though anything came of the break-ins when I was in San Antonio.''

Jake's expression clouded.

''What is it?''

''I think there's a bigger picture you haven't considered.''

Puzzled, she glanced at him. ''I don't understand.''

''Brynn, someone wants something you have.''

She thought of all the anguished time she'd spent wondering why her house had been burgled, why her sense of safety had been shattered. "But I haven't got anything!"

"You *think* you don't. If it were obvious, the intruders would have taken it long ago."

"We weren't wealthy. We were comfortable, yes. But I didn't have expensive jewelry or art work. And the police examined literally every photo and bit of film that was left."

"Maybe we're just not seeing it."

"Seeing what? When my house was ransacked, anything that could have possibly been a hideaway was broken or torn apart. My grandmother's jewelry, which has only sentimental value, was in our safe-deposit box, along with a few bonds. I truly can't imagine anything we owned to be worth stealing, certainly not worth following me from house to house. It simply doesn't make sense."

"And you're certain there wasn't anything Kirk didn't tell you?"

She felt the sting of tears. "He was a *good* man! And he loved Sarah too much to ever compromise her safety. After she was born, Kirk gave up traveling. He said there were a million shots begging to be taken within our own city. So, if you're thinking he smuggled diamonds or drugs, you're wrong!"

"Could he have gotten into something that was over his head? Something he wouldn't have wanted to tell you?"

"He didn't have a gambling problem. Our finances were good. And if you're suggesting another woman, she'd hardly be following me."

"Another woman?" He gently grasped her shoulders. "With you as his wife? Not possible."

She felt her lips tremble. "Oh?"

"What man in his right mind would want anything else?"

Searching his eyes, she wondered if he truly meant the words. He lifted one hand to smooth her hair. "I'm sorry. I didn't mean to stir up painful memories. We'll figure out what was behind the break-ins. But I want you to promise me something."

"What?"

"Don't stop believing in your own judgment or in Kirk."

Pressing her lips together, she nodded.

"You're special, Brynn Alder. More special than you realize."

Uncertainty fluttered within her. But she couldn't be sure if it came from her own doubts or the promise he had extracted.

CHAPTER THIRTEEN

OUT BY THE STABLES, Jake reached for his cell phone. He didn't want to get too far from the house, but he needed privacy for this call.

Too much wasn't adding up. Brynn believed she had nothing left worth stealing. Yet someone thought otherwise. Then there was the extraordinary coincidence of two deaths in her family within three months. Even if Kirk's death was accidental, Jake still couldn't believe that Sarah would commit suicide.

Since Brynn had first mentioned Sarah's death, he had been gathering as much information about the girl as possible. And everything Brynn revealed about her daughter convinced him that she'd been too sensitive to her mother's pain to take her own life. It didn't make sense that she would have abandoned her mother after sharing the pain of their loss until that point. Sarah had gone hiking, a bright, sensible preteen who demonstrated her love for her mother daily. How did that turn into suicide?

Which left two other options. Accident or murder. But what could be so valuable it justified killing a child?

Around him there was only peace, except for the neighing of the horses, the faint sounds of birds. Was the feeling of security only a deception? Was he crazy not to get Andrea out of here? Or was he inventing motive where none existed?

Without his work to occupy his thoughts, Jake worried that he might be giving Brynn's belief in intruders too much credence. And he hadn't voiced to her another possible option. Perhaps she had been followed in the city by an admirer, even a stalker.

In the era of instant information and virtually no privacy, it was conceivable. Information that should be confidential wasn't. But her move to the Hill Country shouldn't have left a trail.

He opened his phone, placing a call to Mike Lambert, Canyon's chief of security. Jake asked him to retrieve an updated report from the coroner on Sarah's death. And he needed to find out everything he could about Kirk Alder. Good or bad, he had to know.

THE FOLLOWING EVENING the ranch phone rang. Jake was up in seconds. However, since the phone was on the table next to her chair, Brynn answered it.

"Don't you ever turn on your cell anymore?" Julia asked.

Brynn signaled to Jake that the call was innocent. "Julia! To be honest, I didn't think about it today."

"Or yesterday. I'm only calling the house phone now because you nearly flew out of your skin the last time I showed up unannounced. By the way, why *are* you answering the house phone?"

"Because Andrea has become quite popular."

"Ah. Must mean boys."

Brynn smiled.

"And that she's better."

"Both." Brynn paused. "Showing up unannounced…where are you?"

"About half a mile from the front gate," Julia admitted. "And this time I *do* have Shipley's doughnuts."

"Great."

Brynn could hear the frown in Julia's voice. "That was said with a notable lack of conviction. What's up?"

"Let's talk when you get here," Brynn hedged. "I'll make a fresh pot of coffee." Hanging up the phone, she turned to Jake. "Reinforcements."

"Great timing."

"It could be. I've been thinking a lot about the incident with Mary. Maybe I am blowing things out of proportion. So far, since moving here, everything's been fine. Now I've come unglued over...what? A plant and a neighbor bringing strudel? Perhaps I need this reality check." She hesitated. "I'm sorry, Jake."

"For what?"

"Worrying you, involving you in a problem that's not yours."

A car horn honked out front.

The interruption saved him from answering. *This was his problem.* If it concerned her, it concerned him.

Jake trailed Brynn outside. As the women hugged and talked, he took charge of the luggage, carrying it up to Julia's room. Andrea heard Julia's voice and scampered downstairs to join them. The feminine chatter lightened the atmosphere.

Jake left them alone, guessing a girls-only evening would be good for Brynn. Strolling outside, he checked around the house. Nothing appeared out of the ordinary. He entered the barn, seeing that the horses were set for the night. As he turned around, the cats ran between his feet. Neither looked out of sorts or skittish, which he took to be a good sign.

Moving on to the henhouse, he peered inside. It looked as though the birds had quietened down. Glancing away from the house and the outbuildings, Jake was sobered by the miles of darkened hills. A thousand places for someone to hide, to watch, to wait.

Jake had stopped smoking a few years earlier, but he felt a sudden, urgent need for a cigarette. Instead, he traced the top railing of the corral with his hand as he followed its circular path.

Staring into the night, he realized his options were narrowing. Jerking Andrea away from Brynn right now could send her back into a downward spiral. Although she was doing tremendously better, her emotions were still fragile. Yet, was it wise for him to keep her here?

Brynn had chosen to believe she was overreacting, but he didn't think so. Then again, they had no solid proof of trouble. He needed that information about Kirk Alder. And he needed it soon. Glancing back at the house, he realized there might be a more immediate source. One who had just conveniently dropped in.

THE FOLLOWING DAY Jake chafed as the hours passed. Julia and Brynn were practically inseparable, and Andrea was their shadow.

It wasn't until well after dinner that they headed in separate directions. Brynn went upstairs with Andrea to help get her ready for bed. And Julia walked outside, seeking her beloved horses.

After a few minutes, Jake followed. Approaching the stable, he called out Julia's name, not wanting to startle her.

Completely at ease, she didn't jump or even look very surprised. Instead she turned her head lazily. "We're going to have to stop meeting this way."

Despite the nature of his mission, Jake smiled. "I suppose we will."

"Andrea looks good," Julia commented, turning back to Fortune, stroking his head.

"Brynn's worked miracles."

"That's our girl." Julia kept her gaze on the horse. "But I'm not telling you anything you don't know."

"Yeah. She's..." He paused. How could he

summarize everything Brynn had done, what she'd come to mean to him? "…special."

Julia turned so that she could study his face. "So what is it, Jake? What do you want to know?"

She was as blunt as Brynn was tactful. But she cared about Brynn, too.

"Kirk Alder, what kind of man was he?"

Julia looked Jake in the eye. "A good one."

Jake hated to probe, but he needed to know. "Could he have been involved in anything, well, dishonest?"

"Ah. She's confided in you. That's good." Julia paused. "For my money, what I said stands. He was a good man and I don't believe he was anything but honest. He wouldn't have put Brynn or Sarah in danger for the world. Kirk adored them, altered his life so that they were the center. He was always getting fabulous offers from all over the world, but he chose to stay in one place, to be there for Brynn and Sarah." Julia stroked the stallion's muzzle. "I've thought about this for a long time, ever since the trouble began. And I still can't believe Kirk would do anything—*anything*—to jeopardize their safety."

"If that's true, what does Brynn have that someone wants so badly?"

For once Julia looked stumped. "I've asked myself that a million times. I wondered if Kirk had accidentally snapped a compromising photo, but every picture and scrap of film he possessed has either been stolen or put through the ringer by the police. And their financial situation was always stable, no significant ups or downs. Brynn's father passed away some years ago, but there's nothing in her inheritance a thief would want. Kirk's parents died before he met Brynn, but there wasn't much besides a trust for his education."

It was baffling. A puzzle without an answer.

"We have to be missing something...."

"But I don't believe it's Kirk," Julia replied. "My gut instinct says it wasn't him. And I'm not usually wrong."

"I hope you're right."

She tipped her head. "Oh?"

"It would tear Brynn to pieces if the trouble was connected to him."

Her expression turned speculative. "Ah."

He glanced at her in surprise. "Meaning?"

"I'm not the only one here who cares about Brynn."

Jake couldn't deny it. What was stranger, he didn't want to.

"So you're watching out for her," Julia surmised.

He nodded.

"Good. She's been on her own too long. And she's not a person who's made for that. Brynn's a giver, and she's happiest when she can give to someone she cares about."

"She's helped several children."

"Them, too."

He paused, remembering a new expression in Brynn's eyes, one he hadn't completely deciphered.

"It's okay," Julia continued, rescuing him. "You're a man. You can't be expected to catch on too quickly." She delivered the words with a smile that included him in her jest. Then she linked her elbow with his. "Come on, Jake. Why don't we rejoin Brynn? I could use a glass of wine before I go to bed. How about you?"

The night continued to darken as they left the unguarded acres of land to step into the house. Despite the cozy lights, the comforting interior, it wasn't a welcoming feeling.

THE REST OF THE WEEKEND passed swiftly. Brynn, Julia and Andrea pampered themselves with female rituals. Julia had brought enough spa supplies for facials, eye treatments, manicures, pedicures, skin conditioning, hair renewal and other things Jake couldn't begin to understand.

So he spent the time staying out of the way.

But he liked the sound of giggles and the waves of feminine voices as they indulged themselves, glad that Brynn could relax, enjoy herself. His few glimpses of the women involved seeing their faces covered in varying shades of goo. He considered himself an enlightened male, but he felt more like an outnumbered one.

By the time Julia left on Monday with big hugs and wide smiles, both Brynn and Andrea looked happy and relaxed. Julia's visit had been like the wind that blew in after a storm; fresh, ripe with expectation. And Jake hoped it was a good sign.

The following afternoon he was nearly sure it had been. Canyon's chief of security confirmed what Julia had said. He agreed to continue digging, but reported that so far Kirk's dealings had seemed reputable. Discovered at an early age, he had pursued his art rather than building a career, but his financial records were as Brynn described them. The first days of the investigation also indicated that Kirk had been well liked. His only obsession had been his photography, and in that aspect he could be demanding and particular to the extreme. But nothing even hinted of illegal connections.

So where did that leave them?

Jake couldn't get the questions out of his head as the day melded into evening. Sitting on the terrace with Brynn, he watched Andrea play with the dogs. Although his daughter strayed near the outer edges of the cultivated lawn, she remained in sight.

Jake's gaze wandered to the hills that surrounded the house. On first sight he'd thought they looked sheltering. Now he worried that they provided the perfect cover for someone watching their movements.

Brynn seemed relaxed, unworried. She picked up the pitcher of tea, refilling their glasses. "It doesn't get better than this. Cold tea, good company."

And questions. "You know, I never thought about it, but I guess I was pretty lucky when I was a kid."

Her expression gentled even more. "Any special reason?"

"I had both parents. The originals. Until my mother died. That's not the norm anymore."

She looked thoughtful. "I suppose not. It's not as easy for people to stay together."

"How about you?"

"I still have my mother. And she was married to my father until he passed away." As Brynn spoke, she drew her fingers through the drops of condensation on the glass, her thoughts far away.

"Was that very long ago?"

"Sometimes it's hard to believe it's been so long. It was just before I went to college. He always took better care of everyone else than himself. And so he waited too long before he went to the doctor. The cancer wasn't operable, and in the end, he only had a few weeks."

No wonder she felt strongly about a daughter's need for her father. "Was it hard for you and your mother? Losing your security, as well as him?"

"Of course it was difficult emotionally. But my father had planned ahead. He left an annuity as well as a generous insurance policy. He'd even taken one out for my education. It would have been worse if we'd had to worry about losing our home."

"Does your mother still live there?"

Brynn smiled again. "Yes. And I'm sure she'll never sell it to live in a condo."

He hesitated. "Did you stay with her after the break-ins?"

Brynn shook her head. "As much as I wanted to keep Sarah safe, I couldn't endanger my mother. She lives alone and feels good about that. I didn't want to shake up her life for something…temporary."

That was so like Brynn. But the questions weren't getting him any nearer to what he needed.

"Jake?"

He lifted his head. "Yes?"

"What's this about? As endlessly fascinating as my life has been, I doubt that's why we're talking about my past."

He winced. "Busted. I've been trying to guess what someone could be after. But it all circles back to one fact—the trouble began after your husband's death."

Her expression clouded. "I won't believe it's something he was involved in."

"That's why I'm trying to think of alternatives—something maybe you chanced on without knowing."

A flicker of gratitude mixed with hope in her eyes. "Then you don't think Kirk was involved in something shady?"

Jake's eyes remained on hers, seeing the depth of her intelligence and strength. Despite her love for her husband, she wouldn't have blinded herself to the faults of a man she'd married. "No."

Something clean and pure radiated from her eyes. And in that instant Jake realized he wasn't challenging or competing with a dead man. He and Kirk had both been extraordinarily fortunate to find this one special woman. And Brynn wouldn't be who she was if she stopped loving her husband just because he'd died. Her dealings with Andrea demonstrated that she had enough love for all of them. If she was ready.

That was something he didn't yet know.

Unprepared for his own feelings, Jake realized he hadn't believed he'd ever find such a woman. One whose strength was tempered by a sense of gentleness she had never allowed injustice to harden.

The sound of Andrea's laughter distracted him. Still in sight, she romped with the dogs, bringing a slow smile to his mouth.

"You think someone's still after me," Brynn said quietly.

He glanced back at her. "I'm not sure what to believe."

"What's on your mind, Jake?"

He hesitated. "I haven't wanted to stir up painful memories—"

"They're already stirred."

"Brynn, haven't you thought about the phenomenal odds of having two people in the same family die within three months of each other?"

Pain tightened her expression. "Yes. But it's not coincidence. The first factored in with the second."

"Brynn, I'm having a hard time reconciling the girl you've described being capable of suicide."

Wincing, she swallowed. "It wasn't easy for me, either."

Jake took her hand. "It doesn't add up. All the signs of suicide the authorities spoke of…those are also the logical reactions of a child who loved her father and lost him."

Brynn bit her lower lip. "Don't you think I wanted to believe that? But everyone said I was too grief-stricken to see the truth. Not just the sheriff, but my family, my friends. It was so clear to them."

"But that's not who you are, Brynn. You're

not the sort of woman who would ignore her child's feelings. Think of what you told me. You were her role model. And Sarah had to know how much you still missed your father. Yet she could see that you'd handled it.

"Maybe so, but—"

"Who knew Sarah best?" he demanded quietly. "The coroner? The sheriff? Relatives?" He gripped her hand. "Or you? Her mother and friend, the woman bonded to her daughter since birth?"

"I wanted so badly to believe that I was right, that they were all terribly wrong." Quiet tears slid down her cheeks. "But there's one fact you can't argue with. Sarah's dead. Gone."

He grappled for a solution, realizing there was only one. "Come back to San Antonio with me."

WIPING AWAY THE TEARS, Brynn shook her head. "Helping children is my world now." She would never repeat the mistakes that had cost Sarah her life. Marriage and motherhood were behind her. And they had to stay that way.

"Just on a temporary basis until we figure this out."

It was tempting, oh so tempting. Which was

why she had to say no. "If you feel that Andrea's in even a speck of danger, take her away."

"Have you done all the work you can with her?"

Brynn hesitated. "No. But she's so much better. And the final connection is yours to make. I can guide, even push, but you have to decide whether you'll be spending more time with her in the future."

"Brynn, you know I can't leave you here alone."

Her heart leaped. Unable to stop the motion, she reached over and traced the outline of his jaw. "Yes, you can. Andrea isn't the only one who's changed since coming here. Your priorities are shifting. And Andrea has to be at the top of the list."

Brynn drank in his face, the intensity of his eyes. This man, this very special man, had drawn out her strengths as well as her secrets. So different from her late husband, Jake was rougher, brasher. Yet he had taken her breath away, then swamped her with consideration. But second chances weren't in her vocabulary.

Jake searched her eyes. "What are you afraid of?"

Everything. Nothing. "I won't watch anyone else I care about get hurt."

His touch was a balm.

It was quicksand.

And she could accept neither. So she turned away.

"We're not leaving," he announced.

She jerked back. "You heard me. I won't watch—"

"Neither will I." Finality rang in the simple words.

Swallowing, she realized they had crossed a line. One that couldn't be redrawn. And she hadn't even seen its subtle shifting.

CHAPTER FOURTEEN

AT JAKE'S INSISTENCE, they stayed close to the house. Within two days they were all stir-crazy. Andrea was picking up on the adults' concern and, conversely, wanted to do anything but stay home.

"A walk," Jake finally conceded. "And we'll all go." He turned to Brynn. "Let's leave the dogs here. They can keep watch."

"For what?" Andrea quizzed. "I want Shamus to come."

"Actually, Virgil's the best watchdog," Brynn told him. "Molly and Duncan bark at each other and their own shadows."

"Fine," Jake said, relenting.

Andrea shrugged, the preteen gesture indicating he was acting like a weird parent.

Jake took a tall walking stick from the hall tree by the front door. It wasn't the best defense, but Brynn had told him that the gun racks in the house had been emptied after Graham Ford's death, the rifles distributed among friends in the community. Julia had felt no need for them and thought that left in the house they could be a temptation for reckless youngsters.

"Can we go walking up at the picnic spot?" Andrea pleaded. "Please."

That meant driving. Glancing around, Jake found the very normality of the situation persuaded him. Nothing had happened. No strange calls, nothing misplaced. "All right. We might as well take an early supper along."

Andrea's grin nearly made him groan. "I'm putty in her hands," he muttered.

Brynn offered a look of mock sympathy. "I'll help her make sandwiches."

Smiling, he filled the water jug, then put ice in the cooler. He gathered a few old blankets and soon they were ready to leave.

It didn't take long to reach the picnic area.

"No wandering off this time," Jake warned.

Andrea rolled her eyes. "Then can we take our walk first, eat later?"

Brynn caught his eye and nodded.

"Fine. But we stay together," he declared.

"Dad, are you trying to turn us into the Waltons?"

Brynn looked away, but he could see her trying not to laugh.

"Just stay in sight, Annie."

For all her protests, Andrea didn't really seem to mind sticking close. Together they hiked away from the stream, Shamus, Molly and Duncan content to run beside them.

The meadow was quiet, the nearest neighbors miles away. Used to seeing great tracts of land turned over to the newest engineering project, Jake was amazed that so much of the area had stayed in the same families for generations.

The trail grew steeper as they climbed, the hot sun high in the clear sky. And after a few hours they were ready to head back to the shade of the trees. The supper tasted better after their exertion, the lemonade sweeter.

Yet Jake couldn't stifle a sigh of relief when they were all packed in the SUV and headed back to the house.

The yard was empty, the peacocks and chickens nowhere to be seen, when they arrived. "Funny. I wonder why Virgil isn't barking," Brynn murmured.

"Because he knows it's us," Andrea replied.

"Probably." She reached for her door handle, but Jake laid his hand over hers, stopping her.

It was too quiet. "You and Andrea stay here."

"Dad—"

"I mean it, Andrea. Stay in the car. Brynn, slide over into the driver's side as soon as I get out, and lock the doors. Take out your cell phone."

Brynn glanced toward the house, fear filling her expression. "Jake?"

"It might be nothing, but I'm not taking any chances. Andrea, hand me the big walking stick."

Silently she complied, her eyes round with questions.

Jake quietly approached the closed front door. Gripping the walking stick in one hand, he turned the knob with the other.

This time the intruders hadn't bothered to disguise their assault. It looked as though a bomb had gone off in the front of the house. Furniture was upturned, slashed. Entire shelves of books had been emptied onto the floor. Tables and lamps were smashed. Whoever had done this must have been desperate—no longer content with subtle searches. And desperate meant dangerous.

Jake stopped, listening.

Silence.

He knew the smartest course of action would be to leave, call the sheriff from the car. Then he remembered why the silence was so eerie. Virgil.

Carefully Jake picked his way through the debris of Brynn's home. Putting his ear to the wood panel and hearing nothing, he took a breath and pushed open the kitchen door. He saw nothing but chaos. As he scanned the room, he felt his stomach tighten.

The dog was lying very still. Dropping the stick, Jake crossed the room quickly, kneeling beside Virgil. His eyes were closed and Jake gently felt for a pulse. And found one!

Not wasting a moment, Jake scooped him up, then hurried out the back door, running toward the car.

Brynn's terrified eyes peered through the windshield, but she quickly flipped the automatic locks open, then slid to the passenger's side.

"Andrea, grab those blankets, give them to Brynn."

She obeyed quickly, her eyes filling with tears. "Is he…"

"He's alive," Jake replied shortly.

With the blankets spread out on Brynn's lap, Jake laid the loyal dog in her arms as gently as he could. Closing the door, he raced around the car and jumped in. "Do you know how to get to the vet's?"

"Yes. I took Ernie in once." She spoke urgently as she called Mary for the number. Once connected, she described the dog's condition to an assistant, who said they would be ready for Virgil as soon as he arrived.

Jake accelerated on the empty road. Glancing at Brynn, he wasn't surprised to see that her eyes glinted with tears.

"I'm not going to lose him, too, Jake." Her voice was shaky but fierce. "I'm not."

ALTHOUGH JAKE RACED to town, it seemed to take forever. Throughout the drive, Brynn never stopping reassuring Virgil. Once at the vet's, Jake jumped out and came around to lift Virgil from her arms.

She hesitated for a moment, clearly not wanting to release her beloved pet. When she did allow him to take Virgil, Jake felt they'd made a huge step toward trusting each other.

He turned briefly to Andrea, but she spoke first. "I'll watch the dogs, Dad."

There was no time to reflect on her mature, responsible reaction. Instead, he rushed inside, Brynn beside him.

The exam room door was open and, as promised, the veterinary team was ready for Virgil. When the vet and his assistant moved forward, Jake knew it was time for Brynn to step back. She did so, but the heartbreak on her face was like a physical blow.

Putting his arm around her, Jake steered her to the side of the room. "Virgil wants to make it, Brynn. For you."

The tears in her eyes flooded over and her breathing was ragged. "I never wanted to have a dog. Julia sprang him on me, and I was so sure that I'd fail him. I didn't want to be responsible for another living thing. And I was going to take him back, so someone else would give him a better home."

"He loves you, Brynn. He wouldn't have chosen anyone else."

With his words, her strength crumbled. Jake drew her into his embrace, patting her back as she cried, praying that somehow Virgil would survive the attack, that Brynn didn't have to go through heartbreak once again.

Guiding her to the waiting room, he settled her beside him on a small, battered couch. As they waited, her tears eased, but he kept her hand in his.

Jake didn't dare offer her hope, knowing how fragile she was. Virgil had looked critical. And as much as Jake wanted to fix that, he couldn't.

Andrea quietly checked in from time to time, assuring Brynn that she'd given the dogs water and walked them. But Brynn didn't speak. Instead, she stared at the closed door of the exam room.

So much time passed that Jake feared the outcome had to be bad. When the door finally opened, he gripped Brynn's hand tightly.

"He's a plucky guy," Dr. Clark said in greeting.

Realizing that Brynn couldn't speak, Jake

asked what they had to know. "Is he going to make it?"

"Right now, I'd say he's got about a sixty-forty chance. He's had a pretty bad concussion. He can recover from that, but I'm worried about swelling in the brain. He's got a couple of broken ribs, but they're not life threatening, didn't puncture a lung. I'll be able to tell more in the next few hours."

"Thank you, Doctor." Jake exhaled, then turned to Brynn. "Don't give up on him, Brynn."

Still dazed, she looked at him with such pleading he felt his stomach tighten. "What could have happened? Why would someone hurt Virgil?"

Because the dog would die protecting Brynn and what was hers. But Jake couldn't say that. Instead, he just held her hand and said nothing.

An hour passed. Jake smoothed Brynn's hair. "I'm going to call Mary Bainter, see if she can come here."

Brynn's voice wobbled. "Where are you going?"

"I've got to call the sheriff, meet him at the house."

"No!"

"Brynn, whoever was there is gone now. But I need to check things out, see about the other animals."

"Bert and Ernie?" She said their names with fear in her voice.

"They were in the barn this afternoon. They're probably fine. But I'll find them, and make arrangements for the horses and birds."

She looked at him blankly.

"No matter what we find out, we can't go back there, Brynn."

The truth in his words hit her just as the exam room door opened again. Brynn's head spun around.

But the assistant didn't look sad. "Doc wanted to let you know that Virgil's vitals are remaining steady. That's a real good sign."

Brynn slumped against Jake. "He's going to be all right," she murmured. "He just has to be."

Jake met the assistant's eyes and saw that the fight wasn't over. But for once, Brynn didn't have to know that.

Mary Bainter agreed to come immediately, suggesting that Roy could meet Jake at the stable. Jake cautioned her to tell Roy to stay in his truck until the sheriff arrived. Then Andrea took his place in the waiting room, her head leaning on Brynn's shoulder.

Walking to the sheriff's office, Jake felt his anger build as he thought of the scum who would haunt a lone woman and try to kill her pet. When he'd filled the sheriff in on the break-in, Jake agreed to ride with the man and his deputy to the ranch.

It was almost worse seeing it the second time. No regard had been shown to the well-cared-for, well-loved treasures in the house. Generations-old porcelain, along with many pieces of Brynn's pottery, were destroyed. Every drawer and cabinet in the house had been emptied, the contents scattered. Despite the chaos, the search had been systematic. Nothing was overlooked, untouched, undamaged.

And all Jake could think of was what if he'd agreed to Brynn's request and left her alone? Would she now be in even worse shape than Virgil?

The thought made him even madder.

As he suspected, the assailants were gone.

The sheriff remained grim as they walked

through each room. He shook his head in disgust. "What kind of animal does this sort of thing?" He turned slowly to Jake. "I'll be honest with you. I've never seen anything like this before, and we aren't equipped to handle it. I'm going to call the state police."

Jake exhaled slowly. "I'll be surprised if they find anything. There's a professional precision to the damage."

The sheriff stared again at the destruction. "It's a good thing Graham Ford didn't live to see this."

Together they left the house, and the sheriff looked up at the surrounding hills. "Someone could hide pretty easily, know when the house was empty."

Jake nodded as they joined Roy and the deputy outside.

"Horses are in a state. Someone ransacked the barn," Roy told him. "Everything, I'd say, except the individual stalls. Nobody's stupid enough to put themselves under those hooves."

"You find anything?" the sheriff asked his deputy.

"Just like Roy said. Stuff's all been taken apart, thrown around."

Roy tugged at his hat, but not before Jake glimpsed the bleak anger in his eyes. "I called some neighbors. I've got enough room for two of the horses. Oral Johnson will take the others. Brad Peterson will take the birds. And I'll stay here until they're all taken care of."

"Thanks, Roy. Brynn will feel better knowing they're okay." Jake glanced around. "I'd better look for the cats."

"They're inside." Roy nodded toward the barn. "Madder'n all get-out, sitting on one of the rafters."

Which meant a climb.

"I'll help you," the deputy offered. "Got some cats of my own. One of 'em's always off somewhere it shouldn't be."

"Thanks."

With the deputy's help, Jake managed to capture both Bert and Ernie.

Steve Peterson, the man he'd met at the hardware store, pulled up in front of the barn as they emerged, the cats in their arms.

Roy clasped Jake's shoulder. "Steve's going to give you a ride back to town. Brynn and Andrea need you."

"Sorry to hear what happened out here," Steve said, extending his hand.

The outpouring of kindness overwhelmed Jake. Never having time for his neighbors in the city, he hadn't realized their value. "Thanks, Roy. Your help—"

"It's what we do. My cousin Evelyn lives in town and she's got a big old house. You'll need to stay in a place that's close to the vet's."

Jake knew they didn't have the option of a hotel. Walburg didn't have one. It blew him away that total strangers might open their homes to them.

Steve pointed to his car. "We'd better get going."

"Thanks."

As they walked away, Steve glanced toward the violated house. "Wish I could do more."

CHAPTER FIFTEEN

BRYNN WAS RELIEVED when Jake returned. Although she knew the ranch had to be dealt with, she needed him beside her. By one o'clock in the morning, Andrea had grown weary waiting for news on Virgil. Mary offered to take her to Evelyn Bainter's house, and spend the night at Roy's cousin's home to keep on eye on her. Andrea begged to take Shamus along. Mary insisted that would be okay.

A veterinary assistant had helped Andrea corral Molly and Duncan in the fenced area behind the vet's office. Bert and Ernie had been thoroughly examined. Except for their shortened tempers, both were fine. And Dr. Clark had sent his other assistant to check out the horses and birds. Since the community depended so much on its animals, the veterinarian was top-notch.

It was nearly sunrise when the exam room door opened. Brynn held her breath.

Dr. Clark motioned for them to come inside.

Brynn kept her voice quiet. "How is he?"

"Stable. There hasn't been much change in the last several hours. But I'm concerned that he hasn't regained consciousness." The vet paused. "It's been my experience that when we treat our animals like people, they tend to respond like people. Maybe Virgil needs to hear your voice, to help pull him back."

Brynn's gaze stayed on her faithful friend. "I'll do *anything* to help him. Anything."

The doctor nodded, then left quietly.

Brynn started speaking. Words of encouragement, memories, stories. She tried to ignore the IV tubing, how still Virgil lay. Stroking an uninjured paw, she willed him to get better. With everything she had, she whispered to him, comforted him, soothed him.

She felt Jake's hand on her back, his support staunch, unwavering. She had no idea how long she'd been talking to the dog.

"Brynn…"

Afraid to turn her head, she squinted, focusing on the paw she held.

"Look, Brynn," Jake insisted.

Hearing a note of hope in his voice, she glanced up. Virgil's eyes were open.

"Oh, Virg!" she breathed. "I was so afraid you wouldn't make it."

His tail wagged weakly and she badly wanted to hug him, but didn't dare risk hurting him.

Jake walked to the connecting door. "I'll get Dr. Clark."

After another examination, the vet was optimistic about Virgil's recovery, believing the worst was over.

Jake could see that even though Brynn was exhausted, she didn't want to leave. "Doctor, I know it's unorthodox," he said, "but would it impair Virgil's progress if Brynn sat beside him as he sleeps?"

"No. He'd probably get better sooner, actually. But isn't she exhausted?"

"Yes. But she's too worried to sleep."

"I've got a comfortable chair she can stretch out in. I use it myself when I have a patient I feel I can't leave."

"Thanks, Doctor." Leaving him, Jake rejoined Brynn and told her the news.

A few new tears glistened as she hugged him fiercely. "Oh, Jake, I hated the thought of leaving him."

"I know. But make good use of the chair and get some sleep, okay?"

"Okay."

He kissed her forehead. "And I'll make sure the rest of the pack is all right."

Brynn's eyes softened and she leaned forward to kiss him back, her lips gentle against his. When she withdrew, she caressed his jaw. "What would I have done without you?"

She would have coped, he was sure of it. But being needed by her felt good. "Just behave yourself and get some sleep."

Although he wanted to check on Andrea, he hated to leave Brynn. Even for a moment.

WITHIN A FEW DAYS, Virgil was nearly back to normal except for some residual soreness in his ribs. But Dr. Clark said that would pass. With the head injury no longer a threat, Virgil was fit to travel to San Antonio.

Jake was relieved that he could finally pack Brynn, Andrea and the pets into his car. He had spent every night guarding the house, worried that the intruder would find them.

He didn't want to endanger Evelyn Bainter, Roy's elderly cousin, by staying in her home any longer than necessary. He had taken the precaution of parking his SUV blocks away on Main Street, so their presence wasn't obvious. And

Andrea had cooperated by remaining out of sight. The pets had all stayed at the veterinarian's. Still, Jake knew they needed to leave as soon as possible.

While Brynn was wrapped up in Virgil's recovery, Jake had phoned Julia with the terrible news. Not surprisingly, Julia was relieved that all the damage had been done to the house rather than its inhabitants. Jake made her promise she wouldn't come out to the ranch, since he still didn't think it was safe.

Brynn was reluctant to leave Walburg, but Jake had convinced her that it would be easier to hide in a big city. His most compelling argument: she wouldn't want to endanger neighbors who had become friends.

There was no easy chatter as they drove toward San Antonio. Even the animals were quiet.

Once in town, Jake watched the mirror closely to see if anyone was following. But he saw no suspicious cars, nothing out of the ordinary. Still, as he turned onto his street, he grew uneasy. Did the intruder know who he was? Where he lived?

Although Jake had a top-notch security system, he didn't activate the door opener to the three-car garage. Instead he parked in the driveway, leaving the car running, so Brynn and Andrea could escape if necessary. He unlocked the front door, using the coded number pad, then cautiously checked inside. But he didn't find anything amiss.

Relieved, he parked in the garage, then escorted Brynn into the house while Andrea led the dogs and cats to the backyard. Virgil, however, stuck to Brynn's side as they entered the large living room.

"It doesn't seem like a house that's been shut up for a while," she commented.

"The housekeeper's been coming, and she keeps it aired out, opens the drapes. But I phoned and asked her not to come again until I called. Same for the yard man."

"This is another side of you," Brynn murmured.

"What do you mean?"

"This big, luxurious house...signs of your success."

He glanced around, realizing he hadn't missed the place at all since going to Brynn's ranch. It had always been a "place" rather than a home. A pit stop between assignments, a war zone with Val...

"Jake?"

He lifted his gaze, pulling himself back to the present. "It's just a house."

She tipped her head. "Really?"

"When I bought it I was still trying to prove something."

"And now?"

"I'd rather prove I'm a good father."

Her smile was shaky. "You mean that?"

"Dad! Brynn!"

Alarmed, they turned toward the sound of Andrea's voice. She ran into the room, looking breathless.

In a few strides, Jake was beside her. "What is it?"

Seeing the concern in his face, she looked apologetic. "I just remembered Brynn's pottery and something I was working on. We left everything at the ranch."

Jake let himself breathe again. "I know."

"Can we get them back?"

"Not today, Annie."

"When?" she insisted.

Brynn stepped forward. "When we have access to a wheel and materials, we can work on new pieces, Annie. But not now, okay?" She gave Andrea's ponytail a tug. "Are the animals all right?"

"Uh-huh. I'm going to get their food out of the car. I think they're hungry." Then she glanced at Jake. "Was a lot of the stuff in the house broken?"

"I'm afraid so."

"I was making a vase for…the house, but like Brynn said, I can make a new one." She bounced out of the room as quickly as she'd entered.

"The vase was for you," Brynn explained. "But it's probably ruined."

He was touched by Andrea's gesture. "She seems to be weathering this first threat to her stability."

"Mmm."

Jake glanced toward the kitchen. "My refrigerator's bare. The housekeeper makes sure it doesn't turn into a penicillin farm. But we could order a pizza."

Brynn managed a smile. "Something we couldn't have done at the ranch."

Jake could see her distress. "What is it?"

"Everything. I've exposed you and Andrea to danger. I've ruined my best friend's family home, the one place she always felt safe and happy."

He frowned. "You're not taking on the blame for this."

"Can you tell me who else should?"

"The scum who wrecked the ranch."

Shaking her head, Brynn turned away. "You don't understand. I'm out of places to run."

He pulled her back toward him. "Not as long as I'm around."

"I care too much about you…and Andrea. I can't let you do that."

"You can't stop me."

He watched her swallow, then touched the soft skin at her throat. Bringing his thumb up, he eased it over the shadows beneath her eyes. He hated to see her pain, hated that he couldn't make it disappear.

His kiss was gentle, undemanding, ending before he wanted it to. Although Jake wished he could forget the horror of the past few days, he couldn't. So he settled for holding her close while he mapped out his plans to fight back.

THE FOLLOWING MORNING Jake phoned the police. He was put on hold more times than he could count. Finally, he was promised a detective would contact him.

Frustrated, Jake wished he could go to the station in person. But that meant leaving Brynn and Andrea alone. And considering that his briefcase had been in the ranch house, Jake was fairly certain his identity had been noted. He thought of checking them all into a hotel, but wanted to talk to the police first. And at least here, he had a state-of-the-art security system.

Waiting for the police to call, Jake used his other line to phone Canyon's security chief. But deeper digging into Kirk's past hadn't revealed anything new.

A few hours later, Jake couldn't stand it. Sitting around doing nothing wasn't his style. Brynn was keeping Andrea occupied, but the house was abnormally quiet.

The doorbell rang.

He felt his pulse leap. Keeping calm, Jake walked to the door and checked the well-disguised video camera. He'd had it installed to ease Val's safety concerns. He saw a man of about his own age, dressed in a suit and tie. A moment later, the man reached into his pocket.

Jake tensed.

The man withdrew a leather case, then flipped it open and held it up. A detective's badge.

Knowing it could be fake, Jake remained cautious as he eased open the door. "Yes?"

"Detective Hamilton. You called the precinct this morning."

Jake opened the door a bit farther. "I was expecting a call."

"Could we talk inside, Mr. McKenzie?"

Jake glanced down at the man's shoes. Well-worn, they could use polish. And his suit was definitely off the rack. Signs of someone on a detective's pay. So Jake allowed him to enter, pointing him to the living room.

"Can you fill me in on what's happened since Mrs. Alder moved away?"

Jake felt his gut tighten with suspicion. "What do you know about that?"

"I knew Kirk Alder at school. We hadn't stayed in close touch, but he was a friend. When I heard about your call today, when Brynn's name was mentioned, I asked to do the follow-up."

"So, you investigated the break-ins?"

"Unfortunately, no. I'm city. Brynn lived in the county, out of my jurisdiction. I read the official reports, but they didn't tell me anything. You mentioned another intrusion in…Walburg, is it?"

Jake knew he wasn't revealing anything the

assailant wouldn't already know. So he filled in the details.

Hamilton scribbled them down in his notebook. Then he glanced up. "Mr. McKenzie, may I ask how you know Brynn?"

Jake collected his thoughts. "She's working with my daughter, part of her program to help troubled teens."

The detective continued looking at him with interest.

And Jake felt safe elaborating. "It's something she's done since Sarah's death."

Hamilton sighed heavily. "I've got three kids of my own. Losing one of them would kill me."

"Did you work on that investigation?"

"Again, city versus county. Sarah's death was in the sheriff's jurisdiction."

Another stone wall. "Then I guess you didn't work on Kirk Alder's case, either."

The other man looked up. "Actually, I did."

"What did you find out?"

"We did a thorough investigation, but finally concluded it was an accidental hit-and-run. One witness contended there had been another car involved, but she couldn't remember the make, model or license."

Finally, a clue. Jake noted the earnestness in

the man's eyes and took a gamble. "What did you believe?"

In turn, Hamilton took Jake's measure. "I'm not convinced it was an accident. The night before he died, Kirk tried to call me. I was on vacation and had my cell forwarded to my desk. I came back to town the next day. And Kirk hadn't spoken to anyone else. But the operator remembered that he'd sounded disturbed. After the accident, I spoke to my captain about the call, but without knowing what Kirk wanted to tell me, we ran into a dead end."

"Did you share this information with Brynn?"

Hamilton shook his head. "She was already carrying an enormous burden, and I couldn't see that it would do any good. I tried to keep on top of things, checking out the reports on the break-ins, but then Brynn fell off the radar. I decided she must have moved to escape the memories. She didn't leave a forwarding address, and frankly, I thought she might be better off leaving the unanswered questions about Kirk behind." He lifted troubled eyes. "Obviously, I was wrong."

"Is Brynn safe here?"

Hamilton met his gaze, but didn't offer any assurance.

"That's what I thought. Can you help us?"

"I'll do everything I can. Officially and unofficially. It's been hard to forget that with one phone call I could have helped Kirk."

"I have some calls of my own to make. If I learn anything, I'll get in touch."

"Same here." Hamilton rose and extended his hand. "I'm glad you phoned."

Jake watched him drive away. Although the car wasn't marked, the plates were labeled exempt, which should mean the car and its driver were genuine. Before Hamilton was completely out of sight, Jake picked up the phone.

Mike Lambert at Canyon agreed to check out the detective. The man's contacts in the police department were invaluable, and better, they were reliable.

Jake's next call was more difficult. He only talked to his father on birthdays and holidays, and he could hear the surprise in the older man's voice at hearing from him. But his father was ready to help.

Torn between his need to protect both Brynn and Andrea, Jake knew he couldn't allow his daughter to be swept into this. Nor could he abandon Brynn.

As soon as he'd heard back from Lambert, he would make another call. And entrust his daughter's safety to another set of hands, his father's.

A FEW HOURS LATER, Jake got the news he'd hoped for. Detective Hamilton was clean. A career policeman, he had earned the respect of his fellow officers. Also a family man, he coached soccer and organized the neighborhood watch. And he had gone to the same college Kirk Alder had attended.

Picking up Hamilton's card, Jake phoned him. The detective agreed to his plan, to escort Andrea to safety and to lay a trap.

Now Jake had to face Brynn, to tell her what he'd put in motion. Luckily, she was alone, with Virgil at her feet. Andrea was in the playroom, trying to keep the other pets entertained.

Jake knelt beside the Border collie, who seemed to be back to normal. "He's looking good."

"He is, isn't he?" Brynn stroked Virgil's mane. "He's been so brave."

"So have you."

Brynn lifted her gaze.

"And now I'm going to ask you to be even more courageous."

"What is it, Jake?"

"We're going to take the offensive. And we're going to start by moving Andrea to my father's home, to make sure she stays safe."

Brynn's face filled with distress. "I've done this. Involved you, made you and Andrea vulnerable."

"Brynn, it's time to move beyond the guilt of the past, to change the future."

"I'm…not sure I can."

"You want to protect Andrea, don't you?"

"Of course!"

"Then I'll ask you to do just one thing."

Her eyes searched his. "Anything."

"Trust me, Brynn. Just trust me."

BY EVENING, everyone knew what to do. Seeing Detective David Hamilton pull into the driveway, Jake opened the garage door to let him park inside, next to his own Jaguar and SUV.

Shamus, Duncan, Molly, Bert and Ernie were quickly loaded into the detective's car. Then Andrea climbed into the back seat of Hamilton's car, lying down so she couldn't be seen.

Jake lifted Virgil, placing him in the Jag as

Brynn ducked down in the passenger seat. The recognizable SUV would be left behind.

After David and Jake were seated, their vehicles shifted in Reverse, Jake pushed the remote, opening the garage door.

Hamilton sped down the driveway, turning west. Jake jetted out directly behind him, turning east. The Jag was powerful, but Jake deliberately kept his speed down. If someone was watching, he didn't want the car containing his daughter to be followed.

Jake drove for miles, waiting for the call from his father, the one that told him Hamilton had arrived, that Andrea was safe.

Relief flooded him when the cell phone rang and he heard his father's voice. All was well and Hamilton had assigned officers to keep watch on the house that evening.

After he was certain they weren't being followed, Jake drove to a five-star hotel in the heart of downtown San Antonio, one that he used for Canyon's important clients. He gave the valet a lavish tip to park the Jag out of sight, then used his cell phone to call the front desk and arrange a VIP check-in under a fictitious name.

A bellboy met them on the fourteenth floor with card passes. Once in the room, Jake locked the door. As Virgil sniffed his new surroundings, Jake pushed a heavy desk across the door.

"Not taking any chances?" Brynn asked.

"I'm a smart man. I know when I have something valuable to protect."

Her smile remained gentle and again she amazed him. Despite the terror of the past days, the emotion and fear of the evening, she looked beautiful. It was the light she radiated, he decided. One that was unique to her.

Doubting she would want to hear his thoughts, Jake walked over to the minibar, then glanced at the wine rack beside it. "I was only hoping for something cold, but there's decent wine."

"That sounds good, but I'd love a hot bath."

"Go ahead. I'll pour the wine." He pointed to a second bathroom in the suite. "Then I'll grab a quick shower."

Brynn looked at him gratefully. He had taken such good care of her. "Okay."

Once in her own bathroom, she saw that it was completely stocked, as he'd promised. She hadn't needed to bring any toiletries, only a change of clothing. And the plush robe that hung on a hook was far more luxuriant than any she owned.

As the jetted tub filled, she looked at her

choice of bath salts and oils. And although she hadn't thought it was possible, Brynn felt herself relax in the aromatic, hot water.

Much later, after she was sufficiently pruny, Brynn climbed out of the tub, pulling on the robe. Entering the bedroom, she saw that Jake was wearing a matching robe. He had lit the small gas fireplace. And on the floor beside the wine rack, he'd filled two of the hotel's crystal bowls, one with water, one with dog food.

She couldn't help smiling. "Virgil and I aren't used to all this pampering."

Jake glanced up, his expression unguarded. "Then you should be." Handing her a glass of wine, he pointed to the bar. "Caviar? Cheese?"

"I'm not hungry."

She saw the understanding on his face and loved him for it.

Loved him.

The truth had sprung free, unguarded. Not expecting to have to protect her heart, she'd opened it—to him.

He beckoned toward the couch. "Then come and sit with me."

Feet strangely light, she joined him, her thoughts jumbled, confused.

"Did the bath help?"

She couldn't seem to sort her words, to blot out the ones that hammered at her consciousness. She actually loved him. "Um, what?"

"Did it help you relax?"

She met his gaze, her own filled with a silent plea. "Relaxed? No...I'm nowhere near relaxed."

He set his wineglass on the side table, then placed his hands on either side of her neck, massaging the tight muscles. Briefly she closed her eyes, the rush of feeling overwhelming.

"You're not relaxing."

Hearing the frown in his voice, she opened her eyes. "No, I don't think I am."

He searched her face, trying to read the shift in her feelings.

But Brynn wasn't certain of them herself. Only that she was where she wanted to be, with him.

Jake's hands moved to cup her head. The kiss began without forethought. But then hunger rushed in. Need demanded exploration.

She was no longer his child's mentor, he no longer simply a father.

Her breath came in staccato bursts as her skin warmed. And she gasped with relief when he pushed the robe from her shoulders, the air nipping her bare skin. But the relief didn't last. Instead it fueled a deeper hunger.

His arms slid around her and he stood, carrying her the few steps to the bed, placing her on the luxurious sheets.

Jake shrugged off his own robe. And the instant his naked skin touched hers, Brynn knew this was what she wanted, what she longed for.

His touch seemed to be everywhere. Her shyness disappeared as his mouth blazed its own path over her body. Trembling, she ached beneath each caress, reveled in the desire he evoked.

Stretching, she ran her fingers over his back, tracing the muscled ridges. As she lowered her hands, she felt him suck in his breath at her touch.

Then his arms were around her, pulling her atop him, their limbs aligned, skin to skin, heart to heart.

Brynn fitted her mouth to his. His taste seeped into her soul. With a sure movement, Jake shifted so that she was beneath him.

Heart soaring, Brynn clung to him, melded into him.

Jake couldn't get enough of her. Although she opened up to him, giving everything, his hunger wasn't satisfied. If he held her for eternity, he knew he wouldn't be satiated, that he would always want more.

Gazing into her incredible eyes, he glimpsed the beauty of her soul, and felt his heart leap. And knew it belonged to her.

CHAPTER SIXTEEN

JAKE COULD HAVE STAYED in bed for days, content to watch her, never leaving her side. But Virgil's quiet whine reminded him they didn't have that luxury.

Still, Jake waited to see the look in Brynn's eyes when she awoke. There was no surprise, just satisfaction, and something deeper. Despite the responsibilities that awaited them, he couldn't resist her lips.

When she kissed him back, he nearly forgot the pressure they were under.

Regretfully, he pulled back, then smoothed the thick hair back from her face. "You're very kissable."

She traced the contours of his jaw. "I didn't dream it, did I?"

"Only if we shared the dream."

Virgil whined again.

"Reality," Jake muttered.

"And you have to call David Hamilton," Brynn added.

He picked up her hand, kissing the soft skin. "The next time we stay here, I'm reserving the room for a minimum of forty-eight hours, and we aren't leaving the bed."

She smiled. "Is that a promise?"

"Absolutely." He watched her cheeks flush a rosy pink. But this wasn't the time for the words he wanted to say. First, they had to deal with the past. Until that was done, the future was too uncertain. "I'll take Virgil out, call Hamilton. Then pick up some breakfast downstairs."

Brynn pulled up the sheet, smoothing it over her arms, unabashedly watching Jake dress. "Virgil might not go with you."

To her surprise, though, Virgil didn't even balk when Jake attached the leash to his collar. Apparently, her dog found Jake trustworthy, just as she did.

"Double lock the door behind me," Jake instructed after moving the chest that blocked it. "And don't open it to anyone but me."

Soberly, she agreed. After he'd gone, she showered, then dressed rapidly, collecting the few things they'd brought along, stuffing them into the overnight bag.

By the time she heard a knock on the door, she'd grown wary again. Recognizing Jake's voice, she flipped open the locks.

But he looked calm, his arms filled with bags from the hotel's café. "I chose what was easiest to carry."

Taking the sacks, she carried them to the small table near the window. "I'm not that hungry, anyway."

Jake unfastened the leash from Virgil's collar. "I know. But you need to eat. It's going to be a long day."

She glanced up. "What did David say?"

"No one tried to get in the house last night. Either they didn't find out where it was or they suspected it was a setup."

Quietly she emptied one of the sacks, aware of the backup plan, knowing its risks. "Did you talk to Andrea?"

"Yes. She's worried about us, but enjoying being with her grandfather."

Brynn smiled at the mental picture. "That's good." She reached for one of the toasted, dark bagels. "What's this?"

"Power bagel—a dozen grains, raisins, dried cranberries. Peanut butter in the middle. But there's a plain one in there, too, with lox and capers."

"And I thought breakfast would be fast food."

He reached into the other bag, retrieving large foam cups. "Is that how you think I'd treat my lady?"

His warmth, sudden and overwhelming, took away her breath.

"Latte okay?" he questioned, pulling back the lid on one of the cups.

Her eyes drank him in and all she could do was nod.

"Mine has a double shot of espresso. Could be a shock to your system." Jake crossed to the bar, unaware that she continued to watch him. "Okay, Virgil, breakfast." He put fresh water in one bowl, food in the other. Turning back, he stopped, his eyebrows drawing together. "What?"

More than she could hope to express. "Thank you."

"You haven't tasted it yet."

"I know it'll be perfect."

Still looking puzzled, he joined her at the table. "You're so certain?"

Oh, yes. "We'd probably better eat. I know you want to get going."

"Right."

Brynn nibbled at her breakfast, dimly registering it was unexpectedly delicious, but primarily considering this very special man and the risk he was willing to take for her.

Jake finished his own bagel quickly, then showered in record time. He didn't check out, wanting to keep the room in case they needed it in the next few days.

On the ride back to Jake's house, they were both quiet. Jake offered his support, clasping her knee every few minutes.

"It's all right to be frightened," he told her.

She knew that, but she hated that he was taking the risk. It was one thing for her, but Jake...

He wouldn't take no for an answer, though. When she'd pleaded with him to let the police handle it alone, Jake had flatly refused. The plan was for the police to discontinue their surveillance on the house first thing in the morning. Then she and Jake would return.

And wait.

Her grip on the car door handle tightened when Jake turned onto his street. The house looked the same—innocuous enough in the morning sun. Hedges, trimmed by a professional, created a faultless border. Grass, groomed with equal precision, looked like an expensive carpet.

No hint of danger.

No impending sense of a risk best not taken.

Jake pushed the remote control for the garage door. He left the door open as they got out of the car and retrieved the few things inside. As they'd arranged, Brynn took her time with Virgil as Jake entered the house through the connecting door.

The police were watching from the house across the street, their vehicles and any trace of their presence concealed.

Jake and Brynn didn't make a showy production of returning home. He didn't leave the garage door open an excessive length of time, just long enough for someone driving past to get a glimpse.

Hours later Jake was wondering if he should flip it open again. Something, anything to spark attention, to bring the situation to a head.

Nerves tight, he had to keep fighting the impulse to glance out the front windows. As they'd planned, he'd opened the drapes after they arrived. Lights were on in various parts of the house, not blazing, just enough to indicate a difference from the previous night.

"Do you think we should call the police?" Brynn asked in a quiet voice.

"Hamilton said not to call unless it was urgent." Jake checked his watch. "It's not that long until we make our first foray." The detective had agreed that it might take a few attempts to flush out their quarry. It wasn't an elaborate plan. Jake and Brynn were to return to the house, stay for a while, then leave long enough for their elusive intruders to strike.

"I wish we could go check on Andrea," Brynn fretted.

He glanced at her, warmed that she treated Andrea like a daughter. "It's not safe."

She sighed. "I know."

When it was finally time to leave, they were both tight-lipped, quiet. Turning off lights, then closing the drapes, they left, taking Virgil along. This time, though, they didn't speed away.

Several blocks from Jake's house an unobtrusive-looking, unmarked car fell in behind them. Their police escort. A few miles later Jake's cell phone rang. The detective in their escort car assured Jake that no one was following.

But that didn't make the next hours pass any faster. It was early evening when, still on the road, Jake called Detective Hamilton. The police still hadn't spotted anyone.

And regretfully, Hamilton's department chief hadn't authorized twenty-four-hour surveillance. If they returned to the house, they were on their own.

"You'd be safer staying at your mother's or Julia's," Jake insisted.

"And you'd be safer at your father's," Brynn argued.

He sighed. "I'm not giving up."

A new determination tempered Brynn's fear. "Me neither."

His jaw tightened. There had to be an end to this madness.

Returning to the house, he and Brynn were both quiet. It was an eerie feeling, knowing his own home could be threatened.

Again they turned on random lights, using the

central computer control in the entry hall, then closed the drapes.

"It's almost too quiet," Brynn murmured, reaching down to pat Virgil.

Jake checked the alarm system. It was on, but he knew a true professional could disarm it. He'd enjoyed the status of having a large, impressive house. At the moment he would willingly have traded it for something easier to secure.

The phone rang, the unexpected sound startling in the silence. It was the sheriff from Walburg. He'd had a report from Roy Bainter about Brynn's ranch. He found that the barn and stables, now empty of animals, had been ransacked again. The sheriff had contacted the state police, who were investigating.

"That explains why no one's been here," Jake told Brynn.

"So today was for nothing!"

Hearing the distress in her voice, Jake took her hands. "It's just one day, Brynn, even though it seemed like a thousand hours. We'll catch them. Maybe not today, but I won't stop until you feel safe."

She shivered. "I never realized I was such a coward."

"You're the bravest woman I know."

"Brave? All I've done is run away."

"You take the chances most of us would never attempt. You've risked failing troubled children. That's true courage, Brynn."

But she didn't feel brave. "I hate all this waiting, wondering."

"Then let's get out of here for a while."

She glanced down. "Virgil, too?"

"Sure. We need to stick together."

While she grabbed her purse, Jake touched the control panel, darkening the interior lights.

Because the SUV had more room for Virgil, he backed it out of the garage. They drove for a while, but the elegant homes didn't hold their attention. Passing under the elaborate arch that led from the neighborhood, he drove toward the shopping center and stopped at the ice-cream stand.

Brynn didn't eat much of her cone, feeding most of it to Virgil.

Jake spotted the uncharacteristic gesture, knowing she rarely gave the pets people food. "You okay?"

"I'm more tired than I realized."

"Then let's head back." He studied her face, noting the fatigue there. "We haven't gotten much sleep lately."

"Okay."

The house looked the same, and the garage door slid open silently.

But as soon as they stepped into the house through the connecting door, Virgil began growling.

The quietly fierce sound made the skin at the back of Jake's neck prickle. Turning quickly, he pushed the button on the control panel that alerted the police. Then he reached back into the garage and opened the door with the wall-mounted control, thrusting his keys into Brynn's hand. "Get in the car, lock the doors and reverse out of the garage."

"But—"

"Now!" Jake peeked into the dark room. Nothing appeared to be wrong. But Virgil was still growling. Moving soundlessly, Jake started forward.

A thump from overhead stopped him.

Virgil ran ahead of him to the stairs. Trusting the dog's instincts, Jake followed. Once in the second floor hallway, he paused, holding Virgil back.

Crouched in the pooled darkness, Jake glanced both ways.

Nothing moved.

Then a shadow fell on the wall. He guessed the man was armed. And Jake wasn't.

Had the man heard him? Or did Jake still have the element of surprise? Banking on the latter, he stood, hugging the wall.

But as he did, he felt the sudden grasp of a strong hand on his arm. Turning to overpower the man, Jake heard the click of a gun being cocked.

At the same instant, he felt Virgil leap with breakneck speed and clamp his jaw on the intruder's arm.

Dazed by the unexpected attack, the man spun about, trying to shake Virgil loose. As he did, he lost his footing on the stairs.

Lunging forward, Jake grabbed Virgil so that the dog wouldn't fall, as well. As the man tumbled, the gun flew from his hand.

Jake heard it clatter on the tile floor below. Virgil broke free, running down the stairs. The man landed, and a second later Virgil had gripped the skin of his throat between sharp teeth.

Following directly behind him, Jake frantically searched for the gun.

"I've got it," Brynn said from the darkness. Her voice was shaky, and as Jake flipped on the light he could see that her hand was, as well.

But she didn't lower the weapon. Instead, she stared at the man who had wrecked her life.

And as she did, the dim sound of police sirens grew closer.

DETECTIVE HAMILTON HAD asked to be on call if anything broke on their case, and he arrived shortly after the patrol cars.

When Hamilton had finished his interrogation, he called Jake over. "Bill Munch works for Edgar Dunbar."

Jake nodded in recognition. Dunbar was a local high-profile criminal.

"At first Munch didn't even sweat, moaned about the dog bite, thought that was the worst of his troubles. But when I threatened to nail him with two counts of first-degree murder, he agreed to talk.

"First-degree?"

"I have serious suspicions about Kirk's and Sarah's deaths, but no evidence. Luckily, Munch isn't smart enough to read me. Said Dunbar was convinced Kirk Alder had photographed him with the district attorney."

Jake glanced at him in surprise. "The D.A.'s a shoe-in for governor."

"Exactly—as long as that photo didn't surface. Too much was at stake if their relationship was made public. A lost election for the D.A., and lost millions in government contracts for Dunbar."

"So that's why they never gave up on Brynn, why they felt they had to keep pressing until they got that photo."

"Yeah. Munch gave me the details. They traced Kirk Alder from his license plates. While the car was parked at the studio, Munch searched it, taking all the cameras and photographs. When he didn't find the picture he was looking for, Munch followed Kirk the next morning when he drove to the police station. Seeing where he was headed, Munch forced Kirk's van off the overpass, killing him."

Jake released a deep sigh. It proved Brynn had been right to have faith in her husband. But it was a horrible ending for a good man. "Why didn't Munch ever confront Brynn?"

"He didn't want to push his luck—he'd already gotten away with murder. So he thought it was wiser to lie low. But with you on the scene, making inquiries about Kirk and Sarah, Dunbar felt they had to act."

Inwardly Jake shuddered, remembering Brynn's concern for his safety and Andrea's, rather than her own. "Now what?"

"Munch passed out when the blood from the dog bite soaked through his bandages. So I had the EMTs take him to the hospital. But I'm not finished with him. Not yet."

BY THE FOLLOWING MORNING, when Hamilton phoned, it all seemed like a ghastly nightmare. Jake and Brynn were back in the hotel room. Neither of them could bear to be in the house. They sat at a small table, picking at the breakfast that room service had delivered.

Brynn stared at her coffee. "It doesn't feel as though it's over."

"Hamilton told me something else, as well. Kirk tried to phone him the evening before his death, but Hamilton was out of town. Now he feels Kirk contacted him because he wasn't certain he could trust the police, either. Not after considering the D.A. wanted to keep his meeting with Dunbar a secret. But Hamilton is also convinced that Kirk was acting to protect you and Sarah.''

''And yet I'll never know if Kirk even had the photo.''

Jake knew there was little he could do to help ease Brynn's pain, the horror of knowing her husband had been murdered. But he could try and find out what had happened to the photo. ''What about his studio?''

''I cleaned it out shortly after Kirk's death, but couldn't cope with renting or selling it.''

''Would you mind going there again?''

She pushed away her untouched plate of toast. ''I guess not.''

It didn't take long to drive to the studio, not much longer to search the space. It, too, had been systematically ransacked. Yet they went over each bit of it again. If the photo had not been found by Munch, it should still be there.

But it wasn't.

Discouraged, they left the sad-looking studio. Jake wished Brynn hadn't seen the destruction.

Now she had nothing that hadn't been violated by strangers.

He slowed as they reached the car. "There has to be someplace else. Somewhere he thought was safe."

Brynn frowned. "We didn't own any other property. His parents are dead, no family home."

"Where would someone put precious jewelry or cash?"

"A safe," she guessed. "But we didn't have one."

It hit him. Simple. Suddenly clear. "What about a safe-deposit box?"

"Yes, but there are only a few bonds and some jewelry in it."

"Are you sure?"

She opened her mouth, then closed it.

"When did you check it last?"

Her frown deepened. "I don't know, exactly."

"Since Kirk's death?"

Brynn shook her head. "No, all the papers I needed were in the desk."

They didn't say much as he drove quickly to the bank. Brynn's key to the safe-deposit box was on her key chain where she'd always kept it. Kirk's had been on his key chain, as well. When the car had been towed away and then crushed, it had probably been destroyed. Even the gutsy Munch wouldn't have dared steal his keys from the car while the police were investigating the crash.

Brynn signed in at the bank with a shaky hand. When the officer handed her the box, it took a few moments before she could lift the lid.

Tentatively she reached inside, touching Kirk's camera, one of his favorites. But no developed photo or negative.

Apparently he'd thought hiding the camera containing the film had been safe, not leaving the slightest clue for someone he thought could threaten his family.

Glancing up, she met Jake's somber gaze, realizing that, together, the two men she loved were still protecting her.

CHAPTER SEVENTEEN

THAT AFTERNOON, released from the hospital, Munch was back at the station. And Hamilton was pressing the man for more.

Jake and Brynn remained in the waiting room to learn whether the camera could provide any evidence. Seeing the detective headed in their direction, Brynn stood up, anxiously wringing the handle of her purse.

"Let's go into my office." Hamilton led them through a maze of desks into a cramped but orderly space.

Brynn perched on the edge of the chair he indicated.

"From the sign-in sheet at the bank and the automatic date stamp on the film, we've determined that Kirk must have placed the camera in the safe-deposit box late in the day." Hamilton cleared his throat. "The day before he died."

It was still so difficult to believe that Kirk had

been murdered. Yet when she glanced up, Brynn saw there was something more in Hamilton's expression. Surely he wasn't going to tell her that Kirk had been involved with the criminals, that she had been wrong to trust him.

"What is it, David?"

"It's about Sarah."

Dazed, she stared at him. "What about Sarah?"

Although Hamilton's voice remained professional, his expression showed his empathy. "Her death wasn't suicide."

Brynn was certain her mind was playing tricks, that she couldn't be hearing this. "Then it was an accident?"

The detective hesitated. "In a manner of speaking."

Brynn jumped up, repressed anger and hopelessness fueling the motion. "I can't take this! Sarah's not a statistic! She was a flesh-and-blood girl—*my* girl!"

Jake took her hand. "He's on our side, Brynn."

Startled, she paused. Yet she had to know. "Then what did happen?"

"Munch admitted that he followed Sarah. There was no plan to kill her. He simply wanted to pressure her into telling him where the photo was hidden. But she got skittish, tried to escape.'' Hamilton paused, his voice still sober, filled with regret. ''And she fell.''

The wail that erupted was primal, an abject scream that told of pain beyond endurance. Sinking down into the chair, Brynn felt the wetness of the tears on her cheeks before she realized she'd begun crying. To think that Sarah's last moments had been filled with terror…that her young life had been sacrificed by these soulless men…

''I'm sorry, Brynn,'' Hamilton said. ''So very sorry.''

She couldn't speak, couldn't take it in. Jake's arms encircled her shoulders, lending support. Fighting to breathe, she wanted to lash out, to punish, to claw past the shards of agony.

Hamilton looked first at Brynn, then at Jake. ''I wish I had different news, that none of this had happened. But I can promise you that Munch and Dunbar won't ever be a threat again.''

Looking as though he wished he could promise even more, Hamilton left them, closing the door quietly.

The wrenching sound of Brynn's weeping

filled the room as Jake knelt beside her chair. "No mother should have to hear what you did just now."

"She was my baby." Brynn's lips trembled, the rawness all-consuming.

"And she didn't want to leave you," he said gently.

Brynn met his eyes, her own desperately searching. "You mean..."

"You didn't fail her, Brynn. I knew you couldn't. It's not in you. It's terrible that she died, the very worst thing that could have happened. But it wasn't her choice."

Brynn's tears flowed stronger, the sobs increasing. And Jake held her, allowing her immense grief to spill into the small room.

Sarah. Child of light and life.

Held in Jake's strong arms, Brynn cried for all she'd lost, her heart breaking once again.

CHAPTER EIGHTEEN

JAKE WORRIED as he watched Brynn grieve. Inconsolable, she accepted the shelter of his arms that night, but she didn't sleep. Instead she stared off into space.

She was traumatized, devastated. And as night slid fitfully into day, he wondered if she would push him away. But with the light, she sought their reconnection, accepting his hand as they walked for hours.

And that night she sought again the solace of his strength. Holding her, he could feel the vulnerability, the anguish. Knowing he could do little else, he simply waited.

Although she was unusually quiet, Brynn did express her need to continue mentoring troubled children. But she thought it was time to find her own place in the country. She'd had enough of the city and the painful memories associated with it. But first she needed to heal.

It surprised him late the next afternoon when Brynn said it was time to bring Andrea home. Reluctantly, he agreed, hoping his daughter wouldn't be a painful reminder of Sarah.

While Jake took Andrea aside to carefully tell her only what she needed to know about Munch's capture, Harold McKenzie sat quietly with Brynn, drinking iced tea. "Jake told me what happened. I'm sorry about your daughter."

She met his sympathetic gaze. "Sometimes I still expect her to run into the room, the way she was before her father died, filled with giggles and nonsense...." Her voice caught.

"It fades after time," Harold told her. "The really intense pain, I mean. Jake's mother and I lost a baby before he was born. She was only six months old, but she changed our lives forever in that short time. And I never intend to forget her—the joy she was."

Brynn could see that Harold McKenzie was a man who had lost—and loved—much.

"I'm glad to have spent this time with Andrea," Harold continued. "I see Jake in her. But he seems different now." His older eyes held a wise look. "I expect that's because of you."

"He nearly lost Andrea," she murmured.

"And you saved her for him."

She glanced up, seeing compassion etched in the lines of his still-handsome face. "Andrea's very special to me, too."

Harold smiled. "I'm glad to hear it."

"There's a lot of you in Jake, as well."

Harold looked both surprised and pleased. "You think so?"

She smiled gently. "In all the best possible ways."

Jake watched them as he and Andrea approached, seeing Brynn's effect on his father.

"Thanks, Dad, for taking care of Andrea."

The older man smiled at his granddaughter. "The pleasure was all mine." Then he winked. "Although this one's a wicked domino player."

Andrea giggled. "Gramps let me win at first."

"Then she clobbered me," Harold added.

Jake glanced at his father, regretting the time he'd lost with him. "Sounds like you need a rematch." He stretched one arm around Andrea's shoulder. "But we need to get going."

Brynn laid her hand on Harold's. "It's been lovely to meet you."

"You, too, my dear."

She fit in perfectly, Jake realized. Saying and meaning all the right things. As she and Andrea walked ahead, he turned to his father. "Dad, I'm sorry I haven't been around much the last several years.''

"I guess that makes us even. I wasn't there for you. And I'm sorry about that. I was scared, you know."

Jake looked at him with a touch of wonder. "Scared?"

"We never talked much about your older sister. You probably thought it was because I didn't care. But I did. It nearly killed me when we lost her. I never wanted to feel that way again. So I kept my distance from you. But I didn't realize until it was too late that it made me lose you sooner."

Jake's hug was spontaneous. "It's not too late, Dad."

Tears glinted in the older man's eyes. "Bring them both again soon."

"It's a promise."

Jake and Brynn were quiet as they drove home. Andrea chattered most of the time, filling them in on what she'd been doing with her grandfather. But she didn't ask any distressing questions. Jake had left out the disturbing details of what had happened.

A sudden silence filled the car when they reached the house, even though the police had taken down the crime scene tape. After Hamilton had told Jake that they'd finished collecting evidence, he had immediately called his housekeeper, who'd promised to eradicate any signs of the struggle.

He'd made one other phone call as well.

As they pulled into the driveway, Brynn stared at the familiar car. Before she could question how and why it was there, Julia opened the front door.

Then Julia was hugging Brynn tightly as she stepped out of the car. "How? I mean…I'm so glad to see you!"

"Jake called me," Julia explained.

Andrea piled out of the car with the pets, greeting Julia, then running ahead into the backyard.

Brynn could scarcely believe it. Jake's consideration swamped her. How had he known that Julia was the perfect person to phone? Brynn wasn't ready yet to talk to her mother and other family members, but Julia… She didn't have to be handled with kid gloves. And Julia had known her through it all, the losses, the moves, the shattering emotions.

Entering the house with her friend, Brynn smelled lemon polish and the lush scents of freshly cut flowers. The table in the center of the entry hall held a vase overflowing with calla lilies, orchids and plump roses. She bent her head, inhaling their perfume. "Did you do this?"

"Nope. Jake did."

Straightening up, Brynn looked for signs of the last frightening time she'd been in the home. But there was no trace. Sunshine streamed in the windows and the onyx floor was spotless.

"That would be Jake, as well," Julia added, watching Brynn's gaze sweep the hall. "The housekeeper's been here. I double-checked everything, but it was already perfect."

Brynn felt her throat clog. "He keeps overwhelming me."

Julia's expression was wise. "I can see why." She took Brynn's arm. "And I'm not sticking around a long time today. You need to be with your family."

"I'm not ready to see Mom or—"

"Not that family. Your new one."

Brynn could hear Jake and Andrea through one of the sets of French doors that stood ajar, leading into the backyard. "You're getting ahead of yourself."

"We'll see."

Remembering the destruction at the ranch,

Brynn gripped Julia's hands. "I'm so sorry about your home!"

"They were only things," Julia replied easily. "And the neighbors have already been busy. After Jake let me know that the bad guy was behind bars, I called Roy, told him we could restable the horses at the ranch. That was all the neighbors were waiting for. The local saddle maker is repairing the leather furniture. Mary Bainter and a few of her friends are putting things back in place, cleaning everything else."

"But it's not the same," Brynn protested.

Again Julia's gaze was wise. "But sometimes that's okay. Things can't always remain as they were."

No.

Andrea ran in from the backyard, her expectant gaze settling on Brynn.

"Why don't I make some iced tea," Julia suggested. Brynn looked at her intuitive friend gratefully.

"Dad told me not to interrupt," Andrea began.

"It's okay. It's your home, after all. You shouldn't have to tiptoe." Reaching down, she gave Andrea a hug. "I'm sorry about all this, sweetie."

"You didn't make it happen."

"No. But it turned your life upside down."

"That's okay." Andrea glanced up. "I'm sorry about Sarah."

Brynn swallowed past the emotion in her throat, glancing at this child who had also become precious to her, one she had come to love. "Your dad told you about her?"

"Yeah. I wish I'd met her."

"I think you two could have been very good friends."

"Really?"

Brynn smiled past the tears. "Really. Like you, Sarah was kind and loving and very lovable."

Andrea gave her a sudden, fierce hug.

Joy, like pain, Brynn realized, could be held close with open hands.

Stroking Andrea's soft hair, she also realized that the issue wasn't about forgetting. It was about how to remember.

THE NIGHT SKY WAS CLEAR, the stars especially bright. Perhaps that was a good omen, Jake speculated as he stepped from the terrace to the lush grass in the backyard.

Julia had left after dinner, and Andrea had

brought the pets inside earlier. Exhausted by the tension of the past days, she had sacked out on the floor of the den, pillowing her head against Shamus, with Molly and Duncan sleeping beside them.

Jake had carried her upstairs, remembering how he'd often done that when she was younger. But instead of rushing off to his study to work, as he would have then, he sat beside her, watching the even rise and fall of her breathing.

He could have lost her. Not by another's hand. By his own. Neglect had nearly cost him his daughter. But Brynn had saved her. Given him back the child he loved.

It had taken that near disaster to bring home the values that mattered. And the people who mattered. All of them.

Brynn stood beneath the tall oak tree, gazing into the night. A light breeze ruffled her long hair, tugged at her blouse. Nearby, the gardenias were in bloom, their fey, sweet scent a reminder of summer's last days.

Apparently sensing him, Brynn turned. "Is Andrea all right?"

"She and the pets are all asleep." He glanced down at Virgil. "Except your shadow, of course."

Her smile was forced.

"Do you want to share?" he questioned quietly.

She glanced back out into the night. "I've been thinking that if I'd only gone to the bank, checked the safe-deposit box, Sarah would be alive."

Clasping Brynn's arm, Jake turned her to face him. "You can't take on that responsibility. It's time to stop blaming yourself."

She clamped down on her bottom lip.

"You said your family pressured you when Sarah died to accept the truth, not to give in to denial. Now, it's valid advice." Jake paused, knowing he had to reach her. "Would Sarah want you to wallow in guilt?"

"My beautiful Sarah…" Her voice stumbled. "No, she would have wanted me to be happy."

Jake took her hands. "I want that for you, too."

Brynn bent her head, looking at their joined hands. "I was about to say the same about you and Andrea."

"She's going to get sick of seeing my face. I'm leaving Canyon Construction. I have enough saved to start a company of my own. Dealing only in local projects, nothing big. In fact, I want to relocate to the Hill Country and I'll be there when Andrea goes on her first real date, when she's invited to the prom.''

Brynn lifted her face, her expression tender. ''I'm so glad.''

''I want to be there for you, too, Brynn. If you'll have me. I have a sorry track record about family stuff, but I'm learning. I had a damn fine teacher.'' He stepped a bit closer. ''I don't come with a money-back guarantee, other than the fact that I'll love you as much in fifty years as I do today. Maybe even more.''

Brynn drew in her breath. ''But what about Andrea? How will she feel about this?''

''I already consulted her.'' He lifted one eyebrow. ''An excellent course in communicating with my child taught me I should. When I asked Andrea what she thought, her response was 'Isn't Brynn already family?' I took that for unqualified approval.''

A wary note of hope entered Brynn's voice. ''But you said you weren't ready to marry again.''

''And you said you'd *never* marry again,'' he reminded her, inching closer.

''Then do you think we know what we want now?''

"For the first time—" he tucked his hand behind her neck "—I have no doubts whatsoever."

She searched his eyes, seeing all she needed to know. "I love you, Jake." Her lips parted.

"And you'll be my lady for all time?"

Brynn's voice was soft, as gentle and graceful as she was. Still, he heard the "yes" as her lips pressed against his. But they didn't need words. Not now.

A breeze ruffled the low-hanging branches of the stalwart magnolia, carrying the silent pledge of their hearts and the promise of all their tomorrows.

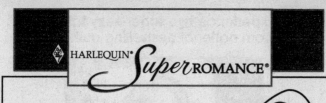

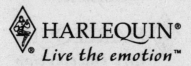

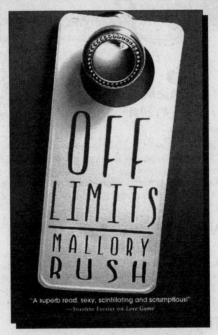
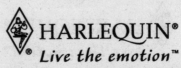

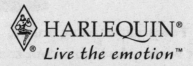

New York Times
bestselling author

TESS GERRITSEN

Brings readers a tantalizing
tale of romantic mystery
in her classic novel...

IN THEIR FOOTSTEPS

Also featuring
two BONUS stories from

Kay David
Amanda Stevens

A dramatic volume of riveting intrigue
and steamy romance that should be
read with the lights on!

*Available in May 2004
wherever books are sold.*

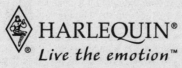

HARLEQUIN®
Live the emotion™

Visit us at www.eHarlequin.com

PHGDS621

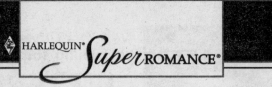

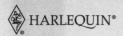
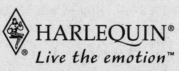

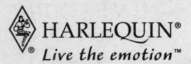